Suspended Beliefs

BEN SYDNEY

First Published in Great Britain by B.Sydney
2023

Cover background image: www.bemmie.co.uk

Cover vector image: www.bigstockphoto.com

bensydney.wordpress.com

ISBN: 9798851028212

Dedication

For Lauren.

For opening me up to a world of possibilities

Epigraph

Good Students suspend disbelief;
great students suspend belief.

When we regularly suspend belief, we set aside our own beliefs and accept the beliefs of others as truths, and then we consider the possibilities that exist in our current reality.

Jody Rust

Table of Contents

Acknowledgements

As a first attempt at creative writing and romantic and erotic fiction, I had concerns that it might not prove to be high quality or perhaps found too risqué.
So, many thanks go to Lauren, for reading and loving the initial text written as the ideas grew, providing much needed encouragement. Her own published novels have been an inspiration for writing this tale.
As have been those from the authors Tee and Monika, creating the desire to actually turn this story into a book. Thanks also to my friends for 'thought experiments', along with everyone else who at some point in their lives have generated the seeds of ideas for elements contained in this purely fictional story.

1 GIFT

Mike expertly reversed his Tanzanite Blue Metallic BMW 3 Series Touring into a space. As he came to a stop, a slight clang sounded from his bicycle which was laid out inside the vehicle and taking up most of the internal space, with rear seats folded down. Getting out, he thumbed the remote close on his keys to lock up, and marched with purpose towards the entrance of the service area building. As he did so, he glanced at his watch; perfect timing he thought. Enough time for a quick purchase and then arrive at his planned rendezvous on schedule.

Once in the little boutique shop he knew was there, it didn't take him long to find what he wanted, in the staffed-by-one and otherwise empty store. At the till, he spotted the name badge of 'Amanda' on the short but evidently big-boobed sales assistant. She smiled and seem to blush at his purchase choice, but said little apart from thanking him and confirming the price.

He thought about entering into some flirty banter, commencing with the familiar: 'Hi Amanda, are you here often', but thought better of it; he was a man on a mission today, and didn't want to waste valuable minutes. Besides, glancing at her only briefly he had decided she wasn't really his type; a much better 'fit' for his friend Steve, who was always extolling the virtues of large breasted women. For Mike, anything more than a handful seemed excessive.

He whipped back to his car, unlocking it as he approached, and threw the bag containing the purchase on the passenger seat, and swiftly belted up. The engine roared into life and he quickly exited the car park and out onto the main road. His destination was not far away now, but he couldn't see any sense in delaying his arrival. Shortly afterwards, he found the expected junction signed towards the country park, and followed the route for around half a mile to the location familiar to him. As he had anticipated and hoped, the area of rough ground which formed an out-of-the-way parking area for accessing the leisure trail beyond it was empty save for one other car. On his arrival, the sole occupant of the distinctive yellow Audi cabriolet got out, and made an arm sweep in the air in greeting.

This was a favourite location for 'action-man' Mike, as Steve called him, for off-road biking for the pair of them. But despite deliberate appearances, there was unlikely time for that today. Indeed, Steve wouldn't even be joining him on this occasion. And the bicycle laid out in the boot of his car, resting on the picnic rug that Mike now fished out of the boot, was for the purpose of 'justifying' to his wife, Joy, where he was disappearing off to for an hour or two. He allowed himself a faint smile on his determined face at the thought that he hadn't actually told a lie of where he was going. Steve would confirm his story if it was ever needed, which Mike doubted.

"Seems an excessively elaborate deception, to

pretend to be biking when you're not, but ok" Steve had remarked the previous week when the plan had been discussed. "Why is it", Steve asked "that women called 'Joy' are such complete miseries? Dunno what you ever saw in her, frankly. Her boobs are way too small for starters …".

Well, it hadn't always been like that, thought Mike, and if Steve wasn't such a good friend, he might have remonstrated with him about that remark. But since the birth of their child, Joy had certainly sucked the enjoyment out of life. He understood the difficulty and exhaustion of raising a young child, what with him swanning off to work each day as normal as if nothing had changed, but the complete lack of sex with her complete non-interest was driving him nuts.

So today he would have a little not-so-innocent 'fun'.

"Hi Mike" called Julia. Her melodic voice snapped him out of his thoughts and into the moment; glancing properly in her direction now he took in the beautiful vista. She, in her bright patterned floral and loose-fitting summer dress, dark hair flowing naturally around her shoulders, and rather impractical but sexy looking shoes and what Mike hoped to be black stockings disappearing up her legs. Which quickly reminded him to dive back into the passenger side of his car and pick up the bag containing his earlier purchase.

"It's a wonderful, quiet spot, just like you said. And what a lovely day for it", continued Julia. She had such a relaxed and naturally uplifting way about her, in stark contrast to the gloom he got at home.

"And I can see why you like it so much; you can glimpse a view of Clifton Suspension Bridge from over there. You Civil Engineers are all the same!" she teased.

They embraced, hugging and kissing for a couple of moments, then Mike led Julia by the hand along the path that unfolded beyond the parking area. Soon enough, he found the convenient secluded spot exactly as had planned, and throwing down the picnic rug, made a comfortable place for them to sink into. They were hot for each other now. They sat side-by-side for a moment in anticipation, looking out over the sweeping countryside view with the bridge in the distance.

"I got you a little something" pronounced Mike almost shyly, handing Julia the folded over bag. The branding suggested the likely contents, bringing a wry smile to Julia's luscious red lips. Quickly pulling it out, her eyes widened.

"Red and Black" she exclaimed. "Your favourite colours, Mike? Seems this might be more for you than me!" she half admonished him before giggling in her sweet sexy way.

Mike was about to answer her jibe, when she whipped up and off her dress to reveal her lacy black bra and panties, partnered with what Mike had hoped for: stockings. Tights would have been a right disappointment. Mike quickly ripped the tag off the gift and handed it back to Julia; as he did so, she swung herself over and straddled him, locking eyes. She wrapped the garment around her slim waist and joined the fastener together. Rotating it into place, she quickly clipped the four straps to her stockings, and then slightly sat back to show herself better to him.

"Well, is the view completely satisfactory to the Engineer, now?" she enquired in an amused but deep and erotic voice, accompanied by a slight shake of her hips.

"You know I'm such a sucker for Suspenders, of every kind" Mike replied with complete honesty.

2 AFRESCO

Mike reached up with one of his hands, the other supporting his body top half upright, to slide his fingers over and along one the suspender straps. Julia smiled then bent forwards to kiss Mike, passionately, teasing his lips with her tongue. Mike could feel his manhood's stiffness erupt in his underwear, and now the urges were irresistible. Twisting his body while supporting hers with his hands, he moved and lay her beside him. Then swiftly he yanked his smart pullover and the t-shirt underneath off in one combined motion up and over his head, and just as rapidly unbuttoned his jeans and pulled them down revealing his pale blue Calvin Kleins and the throbbing erection underneath.

Clumsily he continued wriggling his jeans off his legs, and over his feet, forcing his shoes off in the process whilst grabbing Julia's arms, touching her breasts though her bra, kissing her lips. Finally, they were both in only their underwear, with Julia sporting the addition of the suspender belt attached to her stockings and still wearing her glamorous shoes. Mike felt his socks now ridiculous and shifted away from her slightly to reach down to pull them both off, before returning his mouth to hers. Now she was on her back, Mike arched over her to kiss each of her breasts just above the balcony bra half cups, then briefly nestled his face between them into the soft beautiful flesh. Mike then returned his lips to Julia's, and, moved his hands to her hips, to then start pulling down her panties.

Mike had learnt a long time ago, in fact had gained 'practical' experience at college, dressing up for audience participation at a stage performance of the Rocky Horror Show cult erotic musical, that suspenders can be worn two ways. Straps over knickers causes a problem for easy undressing, but feel 'safer' for a gentleman transvestite, worried about his 'package' springing out of his pants. Not that was a problem now, as Mike yanked his undies down, revealing his impressive erect cock. Fortunately, Julia had taken the trouble to route the straps under her knickers, which enabled Mike to remove them with ease. At least with a little help from Julia, who slightly lifted her hips whilst also reaching up with one hand to brush ever so gently Mike's dick, giving him a wonderful erotic charge. Once he had got Julia's knickers down to her knees, Mike grabbed her hips and twisted her over.

Julia instinctively knew what he wanted, shifting herself over and upwards into a prone position on hands and knees. Mike pulled her knickers the rest of the way down her legs, pausing slightly to manoeuvre them over her shoes, allowing her now to widen her legs ready to receive him, 'doggy-style'.

Mike leaned over to grab his jeans and remove his wallet; 'safe not sorry' was his motto. Fishing it out from the compartment hidden behind his credit cards, he held the Durex wrapper between his fingers and ripped it open and extracted its contents. He could feel the slippery lubrication on his finger-tips as he pushed the teat out. Now in a familiar practiced motion, he offered it up to his penis, which had drooped slightly with the cumbersome slight delay. Rolling the condom down the shaft, it regained a little of its poise. With one hand pulling and toying with a suspender strap, which he fetishy enjoyed so much that his erection became completely solid again, he used his other hand to guide and offer his dick to Julia's expectant pussy. As he teased the rim with the bell-end he reached around and beyond to finger her clitoris, making Julia give out a moan of pleasure. Mike slipped in and pressed himself fully into her, pulled nearly back out and then switched into rhythmic thrusts in and out. He alternatively fingered the suspenders and fondled the smooth curves of her perfect arse.

Trying to take care not to let himself lose control too rapidly, he was bathed in the pleasure of the moment and could feel Julia similarly rise to ecstasy. Then her orgasm arrived in a rush accompanied by the involuntary squeezing of her vagina, which was all that was needed to push Mike over the edge, his ejaculation rapid and warm and safely contained.

His trusting slowed and then stopped, and shortly afterwards he reached around the base of his member to extract it from her hole and holding it to avoid the condom slipping off and being left in place. Pulling and stretching it like a balloon, he twisted the top over and awkwardly completed a knot to seal the container of his cum. Panting with their enjoyment, Julia sank into the blanket and then twisted herself over, allowing Mike to gently collapse on top of her to kiss and cuddle and enjoy the touch of their bodies.

They rolled sideways and then Mike onto his back with Julia on top of him. Pushing herself upright she stated "I think I can take this off now, especially since these are stay-ups" pointing to the belt then slapping her stockinged thighs, before unclipping each suspender strap and unfastening the garment, discarding it on to the mat. "Not exactly what I would have chosen, certainly colour-wise, but I'm glad you seem to like me in your present" stated Julia, trying hard not to sound ungrateful. They embraced and kissed some more.

Suddenly, the noise of a car engine getting louder signalled the approach of a vehicle to their secluded love-nest. "Oh, my goodness" they both mouthed, looking at each other in surprise and alarm. Rapidly but clumsily, Mike pulled his pants and jeans on, grabbing his socks and wallet and stuffing them into his pockets, and then yanking the Pullover-and-T-shirt combination over his head. "Why does it seem to take so much longer dressing when you're in a rush?" he thought.

Similarly, Julia rapidly got dressed, whipping up her dress and pulled it over her head and down her body. Then she retrieved her knickers and struggled eventually to guide them over her shoes and up her legs and over her bottom, thinking that at least it was fortunate that Mike hadn't unclipped her bra. Finally, she straightened her dress and made an attempt at adjusting her hair, pleased also that she didn't need to fit her shoes on, especially since Mike was making an awkward show of trying to shuffle his bare feet into his.

That done, Mike folded over the picnic blanket,

not noticing the insignificant flash of red and black as he pressed it together and into its carrying form, while Julia picked up the purchase bag. They looked at each other for a long pause, with expressions of amusement and relief. Then Mike took Julia by the hand and they nonchalantly strolled back towards the parking area.

3 INTRODUCTIONS

Once in sight of their cars, they spotted a sportily dressed couple unloading a Pickup and readying their bicycles for a ride. But as they approached, Mike's eyes widened in surprise.

"Yo, Mike! Thought this looked like your car" exclaimed a familiar voice. "Now when you said you'd be out and … busy, today, I never thought you'd actually come here. I guess now I can honestly say I was with you with the bike today", quipped Steve, looking across now at Julia, who was half smiling with a look of slight bewilderment.

Mike was taken a back and couldn't decide whether to be angry, sheepish or embarrassed and so ended up stuttering a garbled "Hi, um, yes"

"And this must be the lovely Julia" continued Steve. "You're in marketing, aren't you? Work with Mike."

"Corporate Branding" replied Julia with enthusiasm, pleased to be complemented and happy to join in the conversation. "Yes, I see Mike in the office quite a bit, though we're in different departments; he's Engineering Proposals", she added. Mike just dumbly nodded, feeling out-of-sorts and tongue-tied.

"Yes, I know" agreed Steve, "he designs and promises everything. Whereas us lot in Implementation Services", Steve pointed a thumb at himself, "actually get things built".

His companion made the faintest of coughs which wasn't lost on Steve. "Oh, sorry, this is …" Steve hesitated a fraction too long.

Butting in, she warmly announced "Everyone calls me Ali", before beaming a sweet, beautiful smile that lit up her face. She was standing holding a bicycle next to her with one hand, and a helmet in the other, which she gestured to, explaining "We've actually only just met, but I'm really into biking so insisted on joining …" she hesitated like he had, and turned towards him.

"Steve … yes, I mentioned I was coming to this trail and she agreed to try it out, what with being so local and all" he explained.

"It was lucky I had a half-day today from the shop I work in at the service area" added Ali.

At that point Mike's attention was snapped sharp, and he and Ali made eye contact properly for the first time. He hadn't recognised her before due to the tight Lycra she was now wearing, and her blond hair scraped back into a ponytail in preparation for the helmet she was about to don. Or the fact that she was now 'Ali'. She seemed altogether sexier and appealing to Mike like this, her amble bosom tightly constrained by the Lycra, which also showed off an overall attractively curvy figure. But as Ali also caught his eyes, a flicker of recognition struck her gaze too.

They both mouthed the beginning of "you're …" with matching quizzical expressions. Ali's eyes flickered from Mike to Julia but then rested for a moment on the bag she was holding, and then a smile broke out on her face as she recalled what had been purchased less than an hour ago. Steve became aware of something fleeting between them, "Sorry, err, what?" "No, it's ok" replied Ali. "I was just wondering if your friends would be joining us for the biking?"

"I'm more of a walker myself" replied Julia.

"What, in those shoes?" responded Ali, glancing down to point out her out of place footwear.

"Ah, no, I err, don't have much time today, just came to take in the vista. I need to be going. But Mike maybe could join you".

Mike shook his head "I should probably be off too".

"Aww, Mike come on, it's still early yet" interjected Steve. Besides, just wanted to show you something on the equipment" At which point, Steve draped his arm around Mike's shoulders, and led him around the back of his vehicle to where his bicycle was propped up. As he did so the women continued to chat.

"Lovely view of Clifton Suspension Bridge from over there, you know?" Julia commenced, an expert in comfortable meaningless small talk.

"Yes, it's quite a landmark" replied Ali, willing to reciprocate.

"Here look at this" Steve loudly announced, pointing vaguely at his bicycle. "Campagnolo Super Record groupset!" And then in a half-whisper: "Sorry mate, honestly it didn't occur to me that when you said about your plans, you'd actually bring her here. I thought you'd end up at a fancy restaurant or something. This was supposed to be just the cover story! And I figured I might as well go for a ride even if you weren't. Hope I didn't, er, interrupt anything."

"Yes, well it turns out Julia's a local too and when I mentioned about us cycling here, she liked the sound of the place, wanted to look, and …" Mike hesitated not really wishing to go into exact details of what they actually got up to, though he figured his friend might be guessing.

Steve thankfully cut him off. "Anyway, what do you think ... Ali, eh? She works at the shop in the service area up the road would you believe, you know, the one we often stop at. Couldn't believe when she said she was into biking and would be happy to join me" beamed Steve.

It was indeed quite a surprising turn of events for Steve, who had ambled into the service area building, dressed in his cycling Lycra, as Ali was just leaving the shop Mike had seen her in earlier.

"Going cycling then" she remarked in a warm and welcoming manner.

"Certainly am, care to join me?" Steve had shot back, intended in jest.

"Sure, where are you riding?" Her positive reply had completely floored him.

When he explained about the nice trail up the road near the country park, she insisted he took her home, being only 5 minutes away, to grab her bicycle and get changed. Ten minutes later they were setting off in Steve's bright purple 'Implementation Services' Corporate Pickup which handily had plenty of load space to accommodate both their bicycles with ease.

"How do you know I'm not a mad axeman?" Steve had asked as they set off, his question trying to make sense of this new situation of a hot carefree woman taking him by surprise and completely out of his comfort zone.

"I'm a good judge of character. Especially ones dressed for biking action" Ali replied. "You can tell a lot about a man from the Lycra he's wearing." Steve wasn't sure if that was supposed to be smutty or not. "And anyway, how do you know I'm not?" she laughed.

Steve showed his usual complete lack of confidence as he quickly confided with Mike about the rapidly unfolding recent events. "Of course, purely platonic at the moment, we have literally just met, but you never know, eh? Just my type I reckon, though with my luck with women I'm not counting on anything"

"Now, what have I always said about being bold and grasping life's opportunities" chastised Mike, giving Steve a friendly poke with his finger and regaining his composure at last. "Well, seems like I should leave you two to it."

"Fiddlesticks. You'd be welcome, well at least for a bit, and it would take the pressure off me thinking up interesting things to talk about." It was Steve's insecurities that had doomed him to a severe lack of recent success with relationships. "And anyway, I see you have actually brought your bike" he concluded, gesturing to Mike's BMW.

"Well, as you know I wasn't planning on much of a ride today, and thinking about it, I'm not sure I've brought my cycling shoes. And you know how mad Joy will get if I roll in late."

Steve's eyebrows raised in recognition and shrugged his shoulders in defeat. Taking hold of his bike, he wheeled it as the two friends walked back to where the women were chatting.

"Seems like Mike's going to miss out on the fun" Steve exclaimed.

At this Ali scrunched up her face slightly, hiding a feeling of disappointment. Yes, she was pleased to be out on the bike and Steve seemed a really nice guy, but his short stature, pale complexion and tufty brown hair was no match for the tall, dark-haired and chiselled looking Mike. In return, Mike gazed at Ali for a moment slightly too long; he caught a sense of unexplainable instant, fleeting attraction.

"Well, next time, perhaps" suggested Mike, intending it to be a remark of dismissal, but then adding "especially now we know you're into cycling" realising then that he had unwittingly promised something more. Mike awkwardly held out his hand, which Ali took and shook surprisingly firmly, while fixing him with a glowing smile.

Julia, now looking to make tracks, moved in for a gentle hug with Mike's friend. "Well, bye Steve, nice to meet you at last. Mike's always singing your praises". Steve shrugged in mild embarrassment. Then she moved over to Mike and gave him a peck on the cheek, not feeling confident of showing anything more passionate in front of the others. "Bye Mike, see you in the office next week sometime, most likely" she said slightly too formally.

"Of course; bye for now, and thanks for coming today" replied Mike, also delivering his parting goodbye a little awkwardly.

Finally making a little wave to Ali and a polite "See You", Julia turned and briskly walked the few strides to her car, as Mike stared after her. She started up her car in an instant, and with a brief toot of the horn she was away, exiting the parking area and drove swiftly down the lane.

"Come on then, let's get going, the trail isn't going to ride itself" urged Steve. Ali without hesitation followed his lead, and with a slight backwards look and a shout of "bye Mike" they were gone.

Mike opened the boot of his BMW, slipped the picnic rug under his bicycle, and sat down on the back edge, pulled out his socks from his pocket and slowly put them on, taking a long moment to reflect, and finding that he felt a little deflated, but not certain why. He had enjoyed the shag with Julia, that had gone perfectly to plan. Being almost interrupted was always an exciting risk of 'alfresco sex'. He smiled to himself at the concept.

But Steve's arrival was a surprise, though if he thought about it was always a distinct possibility. Maybe it was precisely that he hadn't considered the obvious likelihood that was needling him.

And what of this mysterious and bold Ali? What was that, short for Alison, he supposed. So, what was with the name badge he spied in the shop. What was it? Amanda, yes, he recalled it as the name of his first proper girlfriend, he wouldn't mistake that. Maybe lots of shop girls go by a different name when working, to avoid unwanted admirers; he'd never really considered that before. But then she said "everyone calls me Ali" which almost implied that's not actually her name.

And beyond that, Steve picking up a girl, at the services; now that was amazing. He smiled again. Sounds like she picked him up he mused. He should feel really happy for his unlucky-in-love friend. But instead, he couldn't help a mild feeling of jealously, which he cursed himself for such outrageous thinking.

Mike hadn't really given her a serious thought when she was serving him in her frumpy uniform. But there was something about her now, something between them in their brief meeting a few moments ago, that really piqued his interest. He shook his head, and thinking that perhaps he had somehow squandered an opportunity, got in the car and started driving, with his thoughts still tumbling. He realised there was a feeling of regret at missing out. Why hadn't he gone for a quick ride with them? He would have enjoyed that. Pity he hadn't had more time with Julia, too. Now he was heading back to Joy, who most likely would be in a dark mood; always she was worse when he had gone out enjoying himself.

To be expected, he supposed, when one of them needed to be engaged in child care duties at all times, and to be honest it was almost always her. And then not-quite-hidden underneath it all, the slight feeling of self-loathing at the deception and betrayal, which he thought he was immune to when he had told himself it was only a bit of harmless 'fun'.

Julia shortly arrived outside her flat in Riverside Court. She couldn't quite believe she had experienced the excitement of the events of earlier, and despite the swift departure, felt good about the experience. What a rush to be fucking outside, and nearly get caught, and then have to dress in a hurry! She reached across to the passenger seat and fetched the purchase bag and smiled. How funny Mike is getting so horny about suspenders like that she mused. She put her hand inside the bag to pull out the sexy garment, but instead of finding it where she had assumed Mike had scooped up and placed it, her fingers found something slimy and cold. "Yuk" she thought.

4 DISCOVERY

"Where is it?" cried Joy, exasperated, searching in the hall cupboard.

"Where's what?" answered Mike, from the Kitchen, who hadn't been paying attention to what his wife was doing. He was enjoying the fact that he didn't need to go into the office today, and was leisurely breakfasting while catching up on work matters, absorbed by his laptop.

"The bloody picnic rug" replied Joy. "I'm going to the 'Bumps and Babes' picnic today, and I need it". Joy had everything ready apart from this missing item. She had already applied just the right amount of make-up for looking pretty yet casual, with clothing to match of a practical blouse and comfortable trousers; smart but most importantly washable, to convey a look of relaxed mum in control. If Mike had been observing her better he would have noticed his wife's still stunning beauty shining through, with her tall frame, back to being slim after pregnancy, perfect boobs that had recovered from the demands of breastfeeding (thankfully behind her now), and wonderfully shining dark hair despite the rather severe looking 'bob'.

"Oh yeah, I think it's still in my car" admitted

Mike.

"Oh, for Christ's sake, what the hell is it doing in there?" Joy fumed.

"Yeah, it was protecting the inside of the car from my bike" explained Mike. "I'll go and get it" he said, but didn't make an instant move, continuing to sip his coffee while reading his emails, distracted.

"No, don't bother" ordered Joy, as she grabbed the BMW keys off the hanging hook in the hall. "I can tell you're busy. Don't know why you can't get a plastic sheet or something instead of using my nice rug" she muttered.

Opening the boot of the car, she was relieved to see the folded rug sitting square in the centre of the otherwise empty space.

"Why he didn't take it out when he removed his bicycle?" she thought, annoyed. "And what a poor job of folding it he's made". Joy unclipped the rug, unfolded it and shook it hard, then smoothed it back into its proper shape which folded up nicely into a handy carrying shape if you did it right, reclosing the fastener. Something bright red and black had pinged out into the open boot as she had shaken the rug, which caught her eye, wondering what it was. Fishing it out of the boot, she held it up. Her puzzlement turned to incredulity as her eyes widened, and then to boiling anger. She slammed the boot and turned, marching with determination back into the house, picnic rug in one hand, keys and garment in the other.

"Michael!" she uttered, not quite loud enough to disturb him from his work. "WHAT THE FUCK IS THIS?" she shouted. That had the desired effect, causing Mike to jump up from the computer, nearly toppling his coffee cup in the process, as he turned and looked though the open kitchen door to see Joy standing in the hall, holding aloft the suspender belt.

All the colour drained out Mike's face as his eyes bulged, and then he felt the flush of heat of embarrassment, followed by a scramble of rapid thoughts as his brain tried to quickly find a passable explanation. He had been in difficult to explain situations before, but this was a tough one for sure.

"Looks like a woman's underwear garment of some such …" he stalled.

"I .. know .. what .. it .. is" replied Joy slowly and deliberately, fixing Mike with a stare that could demolish buildings. "What the FUCK is it doing in YOUR car?" she clarified more rapidly.

"Ah, that must have been left by Steve's new girlfriend when she changed for cycling on Saturday" blustered Mike. Even for him this was pretty impressive on-the-spur-of-the-moment invention. "Works in a lingerie shop, apparently" he added, trying to sound matter-of-fact.

Joy froze for a moment and there was an uncomfortable silence which seemed to last an eternity.

"I don't know what is more difficult to believe, some girl stripped off in your car … to go cycling" Joy finally calmly retorted, "or that 'unlucky' Steve finally has a girlfriend" she snorted in mock humour.

Mike saw a 'pivoting' opportunity. "Oh, that's a bit harsh on Steve" countered Mike. "He met her in the local services and she seems a dead keen cyclist, her bike fitted in Steve's pickup no problem. But it was better for her to change into her Lycra in my car and make use of the picnic blanket to cover herself as …"

"So, that's I am expected to believe, is it?"

interrupted Joy, dropping the picnic blanket, walking into the kitchen, still grasping the suspender belt in one hand, holding her other hand outstretched towards Mike. "Ok, then, I will suspend my belief for a moment … pass me your phone."

"Err, what, um .." dithered Mike.

"PHONE" ordered Joy. Mike duly handed it over. Joy thumbed through the contacts and then hit call. There was a slight pause and then it connected and picked up on the first ring.

"Mike, how are you doing?" answered Steve.

"Ah, Stephen, it's Joy here, it's good to catch you. I trust all is well with you?" Joy smoothly commenced.

"Oh, hi Joy, how very nice to speak with you too. Everything ok?" questioned Steve with suspicion.

"I understand you have a new girlfriend, how very nice for you" Joy continued. "And she likes cycling, that's a pleasant bonus. Strange Mike never mentioned her before" queried Joy, giving Mike a stare, who did his best to look blank, whilst nodding ever so slightly.

"Ah yes, very early days, we've only just met really. Bumped into her at the local services and she joined, er us, for a nice ride. Very keen cyclist as it turns out" elaborated Steve, remembering the important aspect that Mike was supposed to be cycling too.

"Oh, ok, that's what Michael told me" Joy replied, superficially satisfied that their stories matched but still harbouring a feeling of suspicion. "Anyway, you know my Stew that you like? I'm doing it again tomorrow, why don't you join us, say 7pm" proposed Joy.

"Honestly, that is the best dish I have ever tasted,

you know that; I will most certainly be there!" Steve accepted enthusiastically.

"And bring your girlfriend with you" instructed Joy. "I would very much like to meet her, and I have something for her."

"Oh, ah, really? Well … that's kind of you, but maybe a bit short notice and …" spluttered Steve.

"No buts, I'm sure you can be persuasive. See you tomorrow" Joy concluded, hanging up and then lobbing the phone back to Mike, who swiftly caught it. She smiled a cryptic smile at Mike.

"We shall see what tomorrow brings then! You can square off any 'details' with Steve – oh and make this girlfriend of his isn't a vegetarian or something" finished Joy, which sounded more like a threat than thoughtful accommodation.

"Now, I need to get going." At that, she strode into the playroom, and scouped up her son. "Come on Tom-Toms-Thomas, we're ready to meet your friends" she addressed sweetly to Tommy, who smiled and giggled back at her. Everything else needed for the day's outing was already in the hall, now with the addition of the picnic rug, so Joy placed Tommy into the carrying car seat, then picked it up together with the day-bag of baby essentials, a picnic bag with a flask, quality handbag and her coat, though that seemed a bit unnecessary today. Mike moved to assist but was stopped in his tracks.

"I can manage; see you later, dear" Joy said firmly, dismissing Mike. "You can sort out your own lunch, there's bread and apples out, and cheese in the fridge". With that she was out the door like a whirlwind. She loaded her metallic blue Ford Focus with her son and car seat, bolting it into the Isofix mounting points, loaded the other bags either side in the back, then placed her handbag on the passenger side, before getting in, starting the car and driving off swiftly and assuredly. As soon as she was out on the road, Mike called Steve back to explain the predicament.

"Best to go along with what Joy wants he concluded. Can you ring Ali and find out if indeed she can come?" Mike added hopefully.

"Well, if I knew her number I would" replied Steve.

"What?" Mike incredulously responded. "What have I told you about being bold and not passing up opportunities? How can you possibility go out with a girl, in any circumstances, and not get her number?"

"Well, I was just playing it cool, you know?" offered Steve sheepishly. "She said to me that since I know where she lives, I shouldn't be a stranger so I figured I'd call by again soon, given how close we all are."

"Cool? In risk of being frozen out more like! Jeez …" grumbled Mike. As Steve was talking, he had an idea. "Hang on, I'll call you back" advised Mike as he hung up. Opening up his wallet, he fished out a receipt. Headed 'Thank you for your purchase at Wonderland' and printed underneath, a phone number. Mike quickly punched in the digits into his mobile and waited. After a number of rings, it picked up.

"Hello, this is 'Wonderland'. I'm Amanda, how can I help you?" was the reply.

Mike was struck with confusion. The name was familiar, but the voice was different with a strong Bristolian accent he had not heard previously.

"Um, is 'Alison' there, perhaps" probed Mike, uncertainly.

"No-one of that name here" fired back Amanda.

Mike was flummoxed. Thoughts were now spinning in his head. Who is this woman of mystery? Do I really know anything about her, he thought? What is her name actually? But surely at least she must work in this shop?

"I mean 'Ali' … she was working in your shop on Saturday."

"Ah, I think you might mean Ms Wonderland herself" offered Amanda. "Well, she's not here now … but, hang on. Well, would you believe she's just walked through the door. Who shall I say is calling?"

Mike was relieved to then finally hear in a familiar voice the "Hi Mike" greeting from Ali as she took over the call. Confidently she enquired whether there was something she could assist with, regarding his recent purchase. Mike had a strange feeling that somehow, she already understood the situation without him explaining anything. It became clear to him that she had been filling in for Amanda last Saturday, which explained the name confusion. He was pleased that she not only accepted the dinner invitation but seemed completely relaxed about the request, and best of all would go along with the necessary deception regarding the circumstances of the purchase. He also oddly felt that he could completely trust her, despite barely knowing her.

As he ended the call, having fixed up for Steve to pick her up tomorrow, he was left with a feeling of awe about this woman, who seemed to be almost relishing the little adventure. 'Be bold', that's what he was always telling Steve. He stared at the receipt again. 'Wonderland' indeed.

5 DINNER

At exactly 7pm, the doorbell rang. Mike swiftly answered it, and was immediately blown away. In front of him was Ali, wearing expertly applied make-up to present a most beautiful face, framed by stunningly coffered blond hair let down around her shoulders, and wearing a bright red mid-length dress, a side split showing a bit of leg, colour that was perfectly matched with her lipstick, and with complementary black shoes and stockings. Just behind her was Steve, looking about as smart as Steve can get, with a blazer he was clearly uncomfortable in, checked shirt and formal but neutral looking dark trousers. And sporting a smile from ear to ear.

"Evening Mike" ventured Steve. "We naturally got the memo about looking the part for dinning with 'The Richards'" he added humorously, making a gesture with a hand to his blazer.

"Hi, great to see you, do come in" welcomed Mike, recovering his wits quickly. Mike himself was smartly dressed in stylish blue, Nile-Delta open neck shirt, dark blue Charles Tyrwhitt jacket and Non-Iron Tan coloured Chinos. Ali kissed him gently on the cheek, and Steve firmly shook his hand, thrusting a bottle of red wine from his other hand to Mike's.

As they entered, Joy called from the Kitchen. "Perfect timing, welcome, I'll be there in a moment. Mike, take them through and get them a drink."

They slid into the dining room, where the table was already set, complete with an opened bottle of red wine.

"It really is great to see you both" enthused Mike, trying to settle his own nerves more than anything, and wondering what this evening would bring. "I've just opened this lovely red Bordeaux which should go with our meal very well. But of course, you can have anything you like?", turning it into a question with a slight inflection as he finished speaking, and pointing to the bottle.

"That would be lovely" Ali replied quickly. "Do pour me a glass"

"Just a half-glass for me" Steve advised. "I'm driving."

"Sure thing" acknowledged Mike, picking up the bottle, pouring their drinks, and as he did so he gestured to the table. "Please, take a seat." Ali worked her way around to one side, while Steve went to the other, opposite her, as Mike had adopted the end position furthest from the door. No sooner had he poured their wine, his wife entered swiftly, with a casserole dish held between oven gloves, and in an assured manner, placed it down onto the large table mat in the centre. It smelt absolutely divine and mouth-watering.

"Welcome, welcome" greeted Joy. Her entering the room caused Steve and Ali to immediately jump back up, to provide a gentle friendly hug with their hostess, who was dressed in a smart black dress, looking sophisticated with a modest necklace and matching earrings, and lightly applied makeup perfectly accentuating her natural beauty.

"I'll just get the vegetables" Joy advised as she turned and left the room, adding "yes, please", pointing to her glass. Mike duly moved over to her place and poured the wine for her, and then returned to his seat and did likewise for himself.

Once all seated, Joy served each of them a portion of the beef casserole and encouraged them to help themselves to the side dishes of Hasselback potatoes, French beans, peas and carrots. Tucking in, they all found the food to be as good as it smelt.

"This is wonderful, you have surpassed yourself again" complimented Steve; Ali and Mike added their own good words.

"Well, there are a few secret ingredients I have added, like a little spoonful of red currant jelly, and of course plenty of cream" mused Joy "but it seems I can't go wrong with this recipe."

There was some natural small talk as they dined.

"So Mr. Martin, how are things in the important world of IS?" questioned Mike, thinking the exaggerated formal tone Steve would appreciate as an invitation to offload his latest worries, knowing that he had been harbouring concerns for a while.

"Not exactly great" moaned Steve. "Now they've put me on the support call-out rota, thanks in part to those 'dodgy' temporary generators they decided to deploy on sites."

"Sounds like you need to tell me all about it. Maybe over a beer, Friday night?" Mike ventured.

"Oh?" exclaimed Steve, who couldn't help sounding slightly surprised, as he glanced sideways to

Joy. He knew it was difficult these days for Mike to 'escape' out when he was needed at home for family duties.

"I'm off to my mum's with Thomas" butted in Joy with the explanation. "Leaving Friday morning, staying over and back late Saturday afternoon. So, you boys should do something"

"Except I won't be getting drunk" added Steve "as there's every chance I could get called out, because …"

"Of the 'dodgy' generators" finished Mike, and they made matching ironic expressions with a raise of eyebrows, a shake of the head and a 'tut' from Steve.

"Where does she live, your mum, is it far?" enquired Ali, shifting the subject back from work to family.

"Cheshire; nice rural location, but not so far from Manchester either. She's been in her 'new' house for a couple of years now, since my Dad died" Joy elaborated, and her shoulders visibly slumped slightly at the sad memory.

It had been a tough for her and her mother Margret to get over the loss of farmer John Jenkins. The farm couldn't continue without him so had to be sold along with the family home, and Margret move elsewhere; though she didn't move far as she'd known the area for such a long time and had a close circle of friends.

John had hoped to leave the farm to his heirs, as his father had done so, but as their only child, Joy had other ideas, and left home to go to university and then become an accountant.

Her mum had hopes she would marry the RAF

pilot she had been seeing for a while, so it was a bit of a shock and frankly a disappointment to her when Joy introduced Mike, and then promptly got engaged. Civil Engineer just didn't seem to come with impressive enough status to suit her daughter she thought, and relations between them were at best cordial, something that Joy had come to recognise. Since Tommy was born, she often preferred to visit her mother without Mike, which suited him just fine also.

Eventually, Joy gently probed Ali for information about herself.

"This one" Joy gesturing towards Mike with her fork "seemed a little unsure of your name, but did seem certain you work in a lingerie shop; is that right?" queried Joy.

"Kind of" Ali hedged. "Actually, I own a few boutiques. Inherited from my mother" she explained. "But I do get involved in the shops' activities, including filling in on the tills from time-to-time' she added, flashing a brief smile at Mike, who felt himself shrink at the reference.

This revelation came as a quite a surprise to the men, who exchanged glances with each other. They had been assuming she was a simple shop girl, though both had felt there was a lot more to Ali than that.

"What, you own a chain of 'Wonderland' shops, do you?" questioned Mike, who then immediately regretted it. He didn't want to give the impression he knew the place, and risk revealing he had been shopping there. Luckily, Joy didn't seem to notice; instead, she seemed lost in her own thoughts for a moment.

"I've got it" Joy exclaimed. "You're Alice Williams … Alice in Wonderland!"

Mike and Steve exchanged further puzzled looks.

"Oh, it's 'Alice' not 'Alison'" mumbled Mike.

"What, the Lewis Carroll character from the children's stories?" queried Steve, the significance lost on him.

"No, silly, well … yes, but not like that" advised Joy, with a note of triumph. "I read about you in a 'young businesswoman' feature in The Guardian, no less. You're famous!"

Ali smiled and slightly blushed at the recognition and praise.

"Yes, well, of course it was my mum, bless her, who started things off" Ali modestly began. "Including lumbering me with the name 'Alice' and then choosing to brand the shops 'Wonderland'. Took me awhile to get used to that! It was however my idea to expand by going for the 'last-minute purchase for an occasion' market by opening shops in service areas. You've no idea how many 'impulse' buys happen when people are walking through on their way somewhere, and no doubt have forgotten to buy a present. Certainly, beats petrol-station flowers!"

Mike kept his head down, focussing on his meal to avoid eye contact at this discussion.

"Really? I'm more of a Rigby and Peller girl myself, going to their factory shop when I can, but as I understand it you've been doing really well" added Joy.

Ali smiled at Joy's comment, and replied "Well, in that case you certainly appreciate fine lingerie. R & P comes with Royal approval." It was Joy's turn to blush slightly.

They were now all just about finished eating. "Well, then" Joy continued "Mike, if you can tidy up here, I'll have a quiet word with Alice."

"Oh, here we go" thought Mike, though he replied "Sure, of course."

"Let me help you" offered Steve. As the women exited the room, the men started stacking the plates and ferrying everything into the Kitchen, where Mike loaded the dish washer, rather haphazardly, requiring a little intervention by Steve, who was more skilled at the art. Mike boiled the kettle and prepared a cafetière of coffee and carried a tray of cups through to the lounge, with Steve following. He pressed down the plunger and poured a cup for them each, as they relaxed and chatted.

From the hall, Joy turned and mounted the stairs, and Ali followed her, up and into her bedroom.

"Now then, where is it?" Joy muttered to herself, facing away from Ali, and rummaging in her things slightly. "Ah yes, here we are. I wanted to present this to you, as I discovered …" announced Joy, as she turned to face Ali, and stopped, open mouthed.

Ali had unzipped her dress and allowed it to swiftly fall to the floor. She stood there, smiling, wearing red and black bra and knickers; an exact match for the suspender belt that Joy was now holding aloft. "Ah yes, thank you" Ali accepted, as she stepped out of her dress, walked over close to Joy, took the garment from her hand and proceeded to put it on, threading the straps through her knickers and attaching to her stay-up black stockings, completing a matched underwear set.

"I'm not usually lost for words" stammered Joy, "but my you're bold, and even though I am 100%

straight, very beautiful!"

"I know you are" replied Ali, now quite close to Joy, and looking deeply into her eyes. "But, why don't you show me your R&P, I would love to see, if you're not too shy."

"I'm not shy" retorted Joy. "But it has been a long time, after having Thomas, you know … since I felt sexy" She sat down, perched on the bed for a moment, hunched with mixed emotions, looking down. Ali came closer, and put her hand gently on Joy's shoulder.

"I think it's time, to rediscover yourself" encouraged Ali.

Joy looked again into Ali's gaze and at her smile.

"Well … ok then" Joy finally announced. She couldn't quite believe what had come over her. But something about the aura of this confident woman, whom she had only just met, had her delving into her 'special' underwear draw, and before she knew it, she had removed her dress, and set about replacing her more simple everyday underwear with her black lacy Prima Donna Aprodisia Plunge Bra, Deauville briefs and Couture suspender belt and stockings.

"Now you are the bold and beautiful one" complemented Ali, and the women both let out a cry of laughter, as Joy suddenly found confidence to strut up and down in her fine lingerie. Then for a long moment, they sat on the bed, gently and barely holding each other, not saying anything. Ali's lips, shining red, hovered near Joy's, as they stared into each other's eyes again. An inescapable moment of passionate tension.

"Let's re-join the men" Joy finally uttered, breaking the spell. They stood up and quickly got dressed, giggling like schoolgirls.

"Yeah, it's not only depressing, it's downright dangerous; 'dodgy' and dangerous" complained Steve, sipping his coffee.

"Dangerous?" queried Mike in surprise, drinking his likewise.

"The basic problem is it's all been a rush, sites haven't been ready and yet they've ploughed on regardless. So, in the absence of 'proper' electrics, they've stuck these temporary generators in, which keep breaking, so they have to have us on stand-by at all hours to go and sort things out to keep the clients happy. But then, they're not really fit for purpose. It's all a mess! I tell you, there's going to be a big issue sooner or later" concluded Steve.

"What can be done I wonder" Mike mused, not really expecting an answer, knowing that this situation was beyond either of their spheres of influence with the ultra-hierarchical organisation they worked in.

"Simple. Leave. Before it gets worse!" cried Steve.

"Seriously?" replied Mike, searching his friend's face for the truth.

"Yes" said Steve, flatly. "But I know you feel the same"

Mike Richards and Steve Martin had known each other since school, kept in touch though Mike's university years in Bristol, and Steve ended up being best man at Mike's wedding to Joy Jenkins. By some chance they ended up working for the same firm, Bristol Engineering Solutions (BES) in the city too. Just rather different departments. Mike described them as 'theory and practical'; Steve liked to put it as 'thinkers and doers'.

Steve was right about the leaving idea, too. Mike had been searching for alternative Engineering Sales roles for a while, and had even found a place, McConnochie Construction, in Glasgow. Bit of a long way away, he had thought on first look. But now it was starting to seem more appealing. There wasn't really anything keeping him in the Bristol area anymore. His parents had retired to Spain after he and his sister, Helen, had gone away to university. She was still relatively local, having taken up a post as an A&E nurse at Swindon's Great Western Hospital, but they didn't see each other much these days. The bigger issue to moving was that Joy now had local friends with babies and toddlers, although she also wanted to spend more time seeing her mum in Cheshire.

Certainly, things hadn't been right in his department at BES for a while, with pressure to rush things without proper scrutiny, leading to Health & Safety (H&S) warnings, and now here were Steve's practical concerns of corners being cut.

"What would you do, where would you go?" asked Mike

"Ah, well, that's the thing" replied Steve. "I've discovered a few opportunities for Telecoms Services. A bit of a departure, but nothing I couldn't handle. Would mean moving to Newbury or Reading probably, though.

"Huh, not as far as Scotland" thought Mike. "Wow, it does seem as if Steve is ready to make a move."

His thoughts were interrupted by the laughter

from the women upstairs. Steve and Mike exchanged looks, both arching their eyebrows.

"Joy … laughing?" Steve uttered in complete surprise. "Well, Mike, you're always telling me to suspend my belief in things going badly, and be open to better outcomes, or whatever that guff is you spout from time-to-time, but … wow, I had never imagined this."

Mike had certainly not expected this either, more than he could hope for. He had anticipated a difficult, defensive evening of deceptive story telling. Now what? Mike leaned closer to Steve.

"You've picked one here, with Ali" commented Mike, gesturing upwards indicating the bedroom. "Anyone who can win my wife round in an evening is special indeed."

Steve's expression changed from a smile to a slight frown, and he shook his head slightly. "She is totally out of my league" explaining his concerns. "Amazingly beautiful, talented business woman, rich most probably and clearly with a magical gift of the ability to melt an ice queen" he concluded with a wry smile.

"But she's here with you now!" Mike countered.

"Oh, come on" shot back Steve. And then in a lower voice "She is here to dig you out of a hole. You're the one she has eyes for. I could tell that the instant you both first met"

"What?" Mike cried incredulously. But being honest with himself, he knew Steve had a point, and the butterflies he had in his stomach that jumped at the thought told him the feeling was mutual; he was finding Ali a compelling and intriguing prospect. Which made him sweat and flush slightly at the thought of what could be, also a wave of concern that his wife was close at hand. "Shush" Mike urged, as he sensed that Joy and Ali were about to re-join them.

Sure enough, Ali came down the stairs, followed by Joy who had noticeably changed into a less formal but still elegant floral wrap dress. As Mike stared and struggled to find words, Steve couldn't help himself to pass comment.

"Decided it was time to dress down, Joy?" he jibed in good humour. "Very nice, it suits you well"

"Thanks Steve; I see you men have relaxed too" replied Joy, gesturing to their jackets they had removed, and the coffee cups. "I decided a change was in order since Thomas will no doubt need me at some point soon.

"Oh, did either of you want coffee?" enquired Mike finally. "There's a bit left in this cafetière or I can quickly make more."

"Ali and Steve exchanged the briefest of looks.

"Oh, thank you, but we should be going" they announced, speaking together and chuckling as they did so.

"Busy day tomorrow, and probably Friday night as well, what with me being on call" explained Steve.

"Yes, I have quite a bit on too" added Ali "But it has been lovely to be here, thank you for inviting us"

Just at that moment, the peace was shattered by the cries of a small child.

"Ah, right on cue" stated Joy, shrugging and rolling her eyes upwards to indicate that she now needed to attend to Tommy. With that, she quickly hugged and kissed cheeks with Ali and Steve in goodbye, urging Mike to see them out, before swiftly disappearing up the stairs.

On the door step, Ali surprised Mike by drawing close and giving him a soft brief kiss on his lips, before stepping back slightly to be able to look at them both at once.

"Well, boys, since you're both free Friday night, my place for beer and pizza!" ventured Ali. "No need for formal clothes this time, we can dress down. Seven-thirty will be fine."

"Oh wow" they both exclaimed.

"We'll be there" promised Steve. "I just hope I don't get called out by work."

"Yes, thank you" added Mike.

"And bring your friend … Julia" instructed Ali, winking. "The four of us can have a lot of fun together. Plus, I have something of hers."

As she spoke, Ali pulled the side split of her dress up slightly, to flash a reveal of one the suspender straps she was now wearing, causing Mike to be once again dumfounded with surprise, and a little turned on.

With that, Ali turned and started walking to Steve's pickup, with Steve turning to go after her, but not before giving Mike a broad smile and a thumbs up.

Shutting the door, Mike wandered back into the living room, flung his jacket over his arm and scooped up the cafetière and coffee cups. He dropped the things into the kitchen and then heard Joy calling him. More quickly, he moved to the hall, and switching off the downstairs lights, he climbed the stairs. Entering their bedroom, he found Joy standing at the end of the room, looking in the full-length dressing mirror.

"Well, I thought that went well, it was nice to see Steve and Ali, your casserole was lovely and …" Mike babbled nervously, not certain of his wife's mood, before abruptly stopping, open mouthed.

Joy turned to face him, opening her wrap dress and letting it slide to the floor, displaying her sexy lingerie.

"Bed, Mike" Joy instructed with a nod of her head. "You can look, but this is too expensive to touch."

Mike quickly lay on the bed, face up, staring at her, captivated, as Joy laughed, approaching him. Slowly and seductively, Joy circled the bed, and as she did so she ran her hands over her body, caressing her underwear, tugging at the suspenders before releasing them from the stockings. She put a foot up on the end of the bed to slowly remove one stocking, and then the next, and finally unclipped the suspender belt. She walked back around the room and placed the items down on her dressing table before turning towards Mike again. As she did so, Mike hurriedly unbuttoned his shirt, sitting up and whipping it off, before laying down again and awkwardly pulling off his socks. Joy walked slowly and sexily towards him again, this time leaning close and kissing him passionately, before pulling away again. Joy circled the bed again, this time reaching behind herself to unclip her bra. She paused for a long moment, suspending it in place while they held each other's gaze. Joy finally let her bra fall, discarding it carefully with her other clothes, revealing her perfect round breasts. Mike in response quickly unzipped his trousers and pulled them down, exposing his black Gap Y-fronts, his erection now bugling through them. Joy approached the bed again, and this time her hands gently touched Mike's body. She caressed his torso before reaching down to his underwear, tugging his pants down to cause his erect penis to spring out. Joy's mouth hovered near and then divided down, her tongue gently licking his bell-end before taking it completely in her mouth. Mike moaned in pleasure. Joy pulled away again, wandering back to her dressing area, turning, holding Mike's gaze again before slowly peeling her lacy knickers down and off. Mike yanked his trousers and pants completely off, and pushed his clothes to the floor. Joy moved more swiftly now, almost jumping onto the bed beside him, naked. She rolled onto her back, as Mike mounted her from above. He knew she only really liked the 'missionary position' and he was happy to oblige. They kissed deeply. Mike's hands caressed Joy's breasts. Joy spread her legs as Mike entered her from above, and began thrusting.

Though Joy had been nervous about their first erotic encounter for some time, she didn't show it. Mike was delighted by this sudden sexual interest, but had an annoying nagging doubt in his mind. He had drunk quite a bit of wine, and two cups of coffee, and the male anatomy being as it is, he really should have gone for a wee; but he had been surprised and swept up with the moment, not wishing to interrupt Joy's 'show'. He naturally therefore had concerns that this would hamper his performance, and the mental worries alone might have had a similar effect. So, he was pleased that Joy reached her climax quickly, and he managed to do so too, shooting his load inside of her. Ideally, he would have liked the intercourse to last much longer, and then to savour the moment afterwards. But then with his bladder pressing down, he really needed to go, so he quickly withdrew, and shuffled swiftly off to the toilet. Then he experienced an annoying delay as his erection had not completely receded, so his body did not at first comply. Especially since he still felt horny and wanted more. Of course, it would have been even worse trying to pee with a full hard-on pre-release, waiting an age for his tool to be flaccid enough to start urinating, and then annoyingly trying to recover the erection again afterwards. But finally starting, it was of great relief; it took time to empty his bladder given how much he had drunk, but eventually he was done. He re-entered the bedroom, with the pleasing thought of continuing their passion, but discovered his wife curled up, sleeping soundly already, having even put her nightie on. He knew better than to disturb her once asleep, and so climbed in bed beside her with resignation. Although pleased that he and his wife were now intimate again, he couldn't help his thoughts turning to Ali. What a fascinating and alluring woman he found her to be. Despite feeling tired from the earlier stress as well as the sexual exertion, mixed feelings of pleasure and guilt swirled around his brain, keeping him awake. Eventually however, he drifted off into a sound sleep.

Steve's pickup stopped outside Ali's cottage bungalow.

"It was an enjoyable evening, Steve" thanked Ali, smiling.

"Well, thank you for coming" replied Steve, winking. "I'm sure Mr and Mrs Richards appreciated you 'helping out'; you certainly made an impact."

Ali looked seriously for a moment at Steve with her penetrating stare. Then she moved over and kissed him briefly but tenderly on the lips.

"Steve, you are such a sweet guy" she announced. "Friday night. I want you to suspend your beliefs, put aside your worries, and submit yourself to an evening of fun"

"Yes, well, ok, I can do that" mustered Steve, bowing his head slightly, totally unsure of the situation and how he should react.

"Good" replied Ali, smiling again. "We must take opportunities to have little adventures in pleasure when we can."

With that, Ali climbed out of Steve's vehicle and disappeared into her house, leaving Steve to ponder where these recent surprising events were leading him.

6 POKER

Mike, dressed in a comfortable combination of Charles Tyrwhitt checked shirt, navy jumper and beige chinos arrived in his BMW at 7pm at Julia's flat to pick her up, enough time he figured to get to Ali's on time. He had a mix of emotions again. He liked Julia for a casual fling, but hoped he wasn't leading her on. Especially now he and Joy were intimate again. Though on the other hand, he also knew he had growing lustful feelings for Ali. Was it possible to carry on with three women at once? Still, this was just a fantasy in his mind, wasn't it? Since Ali had requested Julia's attendance, that must mean she wanted a 'couples' evening, and maybe that meant Steve would be in luck after all. Certainly, he recognised it should be a lot more relaxed without Joy, and he guessed Ali and indeed Steve would appreciate that.

The thing about Julia was she had a wonderful light way about her, she had dressed casually in a loose flowery pink blouse and dark purple skirt. As entered the car, she lent in and kissed Mike on the cheek. As they set off, it seemed as if she had read Mike's thoughts.

"Mike, I appreciate the invite for this evening" she

chattered, "but this is just a bit of 'fun' isn't it? Nothing serious, you know? I'm not here to steal you from your wife!"

"Yes, that's exactly how I see it" Mike replied, relieved, and yet almost feeling as if he was being gently 'let down', giving him a pang of disappointment. Almost to make himself feel better about that thought, he added: "Certainly, Ali is promising an evening of 'fun', which should suit us all". As he spoke, he wasn't sure himself whether he was betraying his lustful thoughts about Ali, and if Julia could sense something. Or maybe it was just that she was keen not to be 'the other woman' when it came to his marriage.

Arriving at Ali's house, they spotted a Honda CB500F motorcycle just pulling up outside. The rider got off, turned and waved at them, before removing his helmet.

"Wow, is that Steve?" asked Julia. She had always been excited by motorcycles, and the sight of Steve in his leathers was a real turn-on. They parked up behind him, and got out of Mike's car.

"Well, this is a bit of a surprise!" exclaimed Mike. "What brings the mean-machine out tonight?" He was impressed at the sight, but had never really taken a personal interest in bikes himself, knowing for starters that Joy would never entertain the idea. Plus, his BMW was a lot more practical.

Steve grinned, and nodded at Mike but it was Julia's broad smile and twinkle in her eyes that caught his attention.

"Hi Julia, good to see you again" Steve greeted, and warmly embraced. Then Steve fist-bumped with Mike's hand. "Well, here's my crazy thinking" Steve explained, to Mike's question. "I intend to have fun tonight, even if I am on the work's support rota. And if I do get called out, I can be where-ever they need me a lot quicker on this than in the pick-up." He pointed to his motorcycle, which encouraged Julia to move over to it, running her hand gently over the tank and stroking the seat in approval.

"Mmm … I'd love a ride sometime" Julia stated, coming across rather suggestively.

"Sure, thing Julia, anytime!" Steve replied to her advance. "Except, not tonight, I haven't brought a spare helmet."

"Really?" Mike questioned Steve, ignoring the flirty riding discussion. "Don't you need, like tools or anything with you to go to site?"

"Yes, but the current policy is always to send two people to any call-out. About the only sensible health and safety measure BES is enforcing" explained Steve. "So, we can use the other guy's tools, unless he's come by bike too!" finished Steve, with a chuckle.

Although it was mild out, Mike didn't see any point hanging around outside any longer. He was keen to see Ali again and discover how the evening would unfold.

"Anyway, shall we?" Mike encouraged, gesturing towards the front door of the house. Mike stepped up and knocked firmly. Opening the door without delay, Ali stood before them, smiling with eyes sparkling, looking this time more relaxed but still stylish in a Duntery olive-green knee-length dress, with her hair this time tied up. Ali beckoned them in.

"What a lovely cosy cottage you have" praised Julia. "So much character, not like my brutally modern flat."

"Thank you; I love it" Ali responded, pleased. "I inherited it from my Mum, bless her soul. So many memories. I guess I wouldn't have chosen a bungalow for myself, but it suits me just fine. Though with the additional shop I plan to open in the North, I've started thinking about moving; I've always fancied living in Glasgow, such a wonderful city."

An almost electric shock of recognition struck Mike at the mention of the place. He had been wrestling with the idea of the new job opportunity, but had so far discounted it in his mind as it was rather far to relocate to, and yet, through Ali's eyes he could suddenly see the attractive potential of making such a bold move. Especially if it might mean further future encounters with this intriguing woman.

"Ooo, Steve, leather, very stunning" remarked Ali, as she gained a clear view of him. And then laughing slightly, she added "I was certain you were into bikes of all types from our ride the other week."

"Ah, yes, I figured since this is a, well, 'more relaxed' evening" Steve hesitantly replied, glancing at Mike briefly, that I'd use the 'more fun' form of transport tonight. Ok, if I leave take my boots and stuff off and leave here by the door?"

"Yes, of course" smiled Ali, winking. "You've certainly got the right frame of mind for this 'fun' evening."

Steve dropped his helmet and gloves, pulled off his jacket, to reveal a "BES" branded sweatshirt, and then proceeded to remove his leather boots and over-trousers.

"Oh no, not the work's dreaded corporate clothing" cried Mike as he looked at Steve's top.

Before recognising his comment might be a little insulting to Julia, since it was her department that dealt with all things branded. "Sorry Julia, no offence."

"Oh, none taken, don't be silly!" replied Julia, who was busy taking an eyeful of Steve as he disrobed.

"Come and help me in the Kitchen for a minute." interjected Ali, pulling Julia away.

"Of course" replied Julia.

Mike and Julia had brought two bottles of wine with them, one white, one red.

"Mike, you can open one of your bottles of wine", Ali instructed, gesturing to the dining table in her open-plan lounge-dinning space, which was already set with glasses, cutlery, a bowl of salad, and additionally, a bottle opener too.

Both Ali and Julia agreed they were happy with either, so Mike selected the red and left the white with Julia to put in the fridge.

Steve on the other hand, had brought pack of four bottles of non-alcoholic Heineken 0.0 lager. "Regrettably, I err, can't drink in case I get called away by work, I'm afraid." At which he passed his bottles to Julia to take to the fridge also.

The girls disappeared into the kitchen.

Steve finished sorting out his motorcycle gear, sweeping a hand through his hair, and casually wandered into the living-room area, hesitating by the sofa while he thought about taking a seat, while Mike busied himself with the wine.

"Do you ever make an effort? Mike asked in jest, staring at his sweatshirt and faded denims.

"I dressed up at your place just the other night, remember?" Steve through back. "I've come as I am tonight. And ready to go to work if I'm needed", he concluded, pointing at the logo.

Mike slightly tutted but then smiled at his old friend. "He'll never change" thought Mike.

There was a burst of loud laughter from the kitchen, followed by giggling that seemed to go on for some time, to the surprise of the men, who exchanged puzzled looks.

"It seems Ali is working her charm again" mused Mike.

Eventually, the women emerged from the kitchen carrying plates and pizzas, which smelled divine, smiling and still giggling.

"Come, sit and let's eat" encouraged Ali. They all sat down and tucked in. Mike filled three wine glasses, and Ali had brought in a bottle of the zero-alcohol lager, which had been cool but had now chilled slightly more from being in her fridge-freezer for a brief few moments. "Thanks" acknowledged Steve as he took the bottle from Ali, and then made use of the bottle-opener, which happily had an attachment for beer bottles too.

They feasted on the mix of pepperoni and sloppy Giuseppe, which was from the pizza express range, together with the salad and slices of garlic bread. The meal went by in a comfortably relaxed way, with easy-flowing small-talk. A bit of 'talking shop' naturally crept in given that three of them worked for BES. Steve mentioned again his dissatisfaction with his job, but surprisingly it was Julia who expressed a desire to move on.

"I'm considering a shift to London, there are a number of marketing posts that would suit me well" she revealed. "I just feel that the working environment at BES is rather restrictive and I could benefit from a move."

Steve and Mike found themselves nodding in agreement. Ali meanwhile had made an efficient job of clearing around everyone as they went, without them really noticing. She brought out another beer for Steve, while Mike kept the wine topped up, until the bottle was empty.

"Ok then, since we're about done eating, time to play" announced Ali, smiling. She gave Julia a sideways look and they both giggled. She reached over to a side-board and produced a desk of cards, together with a box of chips. "How about a few games of poker?"

"Well, I'm in, but you'll be losing all your cash, I know Mike's a right card shark!" exclaimed Steve.

Julia giggled, but then added "I don't have any cash with me to lose."

"Well, that's ok", advised Ali. Because we won't play for money tonight. We can play for clothes!"

Mike's jaw dropped, while Steve nearly choked on his beer. Julia giggled again, clearly having been put in the picture by Ali earlier.

"And I think, a few forfeits will be in order, starting with the first person to lose a hand has to put this on for a round" declared Ali, producing something red and black from the side and whipping it swiftly onto the table. They stared for a moment at the suspender belt now between them, before all hooting with laughter.

"Goodness, I meant to ask what happened to that" asked Julia.

"And how you got it back?" queried Mike, flushing red slightly.

"Melting the ice queen in the process!" exclaimed Steve, exchanging looks with Ali and then Mike, while Julia looked between them, puzzled.

"Well, let's just say I have my ways" beamed Ali, as she extracted the cards and started shuffling them.

"You will have to teach me the rules" mentioned Julia. "I know the basics but some of the more complicated poker play has always mystified me a bit."

"Don't worry, we'll be gentle with you, and can certainly help you … out … with a few things" teased Steve, giving her a suggestive glance.

"Oh of course" replied Ali. "It's not so complicated, I find, as long as you don't get confused by some of the terms."

"Well, as Steve indicated, I like poker" enthused Mike. "But I'm not sure I get how the betting works in, err, this variant of the game."

"I have some clear rules, so let me explain" began Ali. "At the beginning of the game, everyone 'pledges' an item of clothing to take off, for which the 'bank' advances 10 tokens, which you use for betting" advised Ali, pointing to her box of chips. "Once you run out of chips, then you must strip your item of clothing off. And can then 'purchase' another 10 chips to stay in the game, by pledging your next clothing item. When you strip off your last item …" Ali paused for a moment, considering. "Looking at us all, I reckon everyone's wearing probably 4 items each; let's not count socks, they're not so interesting! So, when you have no more clothes, then you're out, because you have nothing left for the bank to advance you any more chips against."

"Ok, right, I see" responded Mike, seriously.

"Yup, I can see Mr. Cards here is taking it all in" jibed Steve looking at Mike's serious questioning face.

"Yeah, well just making sure I understand" Mike replied defensively. "And the game itself, there are a number of variants …"

"Texas Hold'em" stated Ali. "Two cards in the middle, with three dealt on the Flop, and one more card each for the Turn and the River. It's the most fun for betting, though can be a long game. So, to speed it up, we'll start with the Big Blind at two chips, and double it every two hands, so that should bring the game to a conclusion swiftly enough."

Julia shook her head slightly, trying to get her mind around it. "Well, you'll have to remind me of everything as we play" she asked.

"Sure" confirmed Ali.

"Most of all that will just take care of itself" advised Steve, trying to put Julia at ease. "The main thing for you to know is the value of the hands. Then you'll know if it's worth raising, calling or folding."

"Ok, that would be great" thanked Julia, and reached over and squeezed Steve's hand gently.

"Here you are" added Ali, as she turned over some cards.

"Right. So, you see, there's a pair" explained Steve, as Ali had turned over two Aces.

"Yes, well I get that!" replied Julia, showing mild annoyance, hoping that they didn't think she was a complete dunce.

"Ok, then, well this is the lowest hand you can get, apart from just having a high card, like this" Steve demonstrated by removing one of the Aces, and showing four other non-matching cards. "So then, a better hand is two pairs, which is beaten by three-of-a-kind. So that's the first four combinations which will be the majority of hands you'll see." Ali had turned over two Jacks to add to the Aces, and then found another Ace to show the combinations.

"So, these two together" Ali continued, putting the Aces and Jacks together "make a Full House"

"Yes, but before that is a Straight, which is a run of numbers, and then after that, a flush, which is five cards all of the same suit" interjected Steve. As he did so, Ali had fished out a run of 2, 3, 4, and 5 to add to one of the Aces, and then found five cards all with the same suit of clubs.

"Then it's the Full House, and after that, four-of-a-kind" Steve added, as Ali turned over another Ace.

"Finally, the best hand is a Straight Flush, of which, a 'Royal' Straight Flush of Ace, King, Queen, Jack and 10 can't be beaten" concluded Steve.

"So, you see, there are only nine types of hand" added Mike, who had watched with mild disinterest up to that point. "Fairly easy to remember, though I dare say we might end up arguing at some point."

"Yeah, I know what you mean, I often forget for some reason that a Flush beats a Straight, for instance" agreed Steve.

"Of course, within each hand type we will compare the different strengths to assess the winning combination each time" finished Mike, who was now done with the explanations and keen to get on with the game.

"Sure, I think I've got all that, so I'm sure I'll do just fine" thanked Julia.

Ali took back all the cards and shuffled them again

"So then, tops or bottoms?" Ali requested with a smirk. "Your clothing pledge to receive your first 10 coins. Of course, if you want to quit at any time, you can just stop pledging when you run out of chips."

"Well, naturally I am selecting this fetching BES sweatshirt" chuckled Steve.

"It should be our first priority to remove it from you" jested Mike. "And sure, I'll go with my jumper too."

"More challenging for us Ladies" mused Ali. "It will have to be my dress."

"Yes, and likewise my skirt" added Julia, giggling. "At least I can try to hide my lower half behind this table."

"Ok, settled then" concluded Ali, who passed 10 chips to each of them, and 10 to herself too, pushing the box of remaining chips to one side, and then placing a 'dealer chip' in front of herself.

"What's that?" questioned Julia.

"Ah yes, this is the Dealer button" explained Ali. "We will pass this clockwise each turn to indicate who is dealing."

"In the old days, they used a knife called a 'buck' as a dealer marker, which is where the expression 'pass the buck' comes from" mentioned Steve.

"Oh, come on. You just made that up!" accused Mike.

"No, no, it's a true fact, I assure you" responded Steve. "These days the position is more commonly known as 'The Button'".

"Anyway, it's important, because the person left of 'The Button' is the 'Small Blind', who will have to put in half of the initial stake of the person to their left, the 'Big Blind' starting in our case at two chips" stated

Ali. "So, I'll deal first, which means Steve needs to put in one chip, and you'll have to put in two chips"

"They're called 'Blinds' because you have to put in the chips before you see your cards" explained Steve, as he tossed a chip into the centre of the table; Julia followed likewise with two chips. Then Ali dealt two cards to everyone.

"Now the actual betting can commence, starting with Mike, who has the 'Under The Gun' position" advised Ali.

"And is there a reason it's called that then, Steve?" asked Mike, slightly mocking.

"Don't know about that one, I'll admit" conceded Steve.

"Anyway, Mike with his first bet has to either equal the Big Blind amount, or fold. Or, he can raise. In this game, the permitted raise from is restricted to between equal to and double the Big Blind."

"Oh, really?" questioned Mike. "So, I can only raise by 2, 3 or 4 chips?"

"Yes, until the Big Blind increases. Or, unless someone else then raises, then you can re-raise."

"Ok, I've got it" replied Mike. "That's actually a good way to play to stop people ruining the game with crazy large initial bets."

Mike took a look at his cards. A pair of 3s, in spades and hearts. Not bad start, he thought; sometimes a pair can be all you need. Though, quite a weak one. Despite this game being 'very social', he couldn't help but be competitive and wanting to win. Often, he might be tempted to try to 'scare' people away at this early point in the round with a large bet. But he didn't feel like being too risky at the start of the game, not knowing how the others would play.

"I call" announced Mike, throwing in two chips.

Ali glanced at her cards. A 10 and an 8 of clubs. "I call" she echoed, adding two chips also.

Steve looked at his hand, revealing a Queen of diamonds and a 2 of clubs. "Now, as I have placed the Small Blind already, I only need to add one chip to call" Steve advised. "Though I could instead fold, then only losing the 1 chip. But, hey, I'm in. Call." Steve tossed 1 chip into the growing pot.

Julia studied her cards. She couldn't see anything remarkable about a 6 of hearts and a 9 of spades. Except the thought 'soixante neuf' entered her mind, making her smile broadly. Something that Mike noticed which made him wonder if she had a good hand. "So, what's the minimum I need to bet?" she questioned.

"Actually, nothing" answered Ali. "Because you're the Big Blind, you've already bet. So, you can just 'Check' instead. And also, although you could, there's no point folding at this point, as it would cost you the same. But if you want to, you can raise, which would mean everyone needs to call again to continue."

"Yes, I see" confirmed Julia. "Ok then, I Check."

"That concludes the Preflop betting, so now I deal the Flop cards" stated Ali, who proceeded to turn over three cards and place them in the middle. King of Diamonds, Jack of Hearts and 10 of spades.

"These betting rounds have such strange names" commented Julia.

Steve as Small Blind commenced the next round of betting. He thoughtfully considered the position, scratching his chin. He left his two cards face down in front of him; he didn't need to hold and look at them again, he could remember what he had; instead he stared at the community cards and wondered about the possibilities. With what was on the table, he could make King, Queen, Jack, 10. One off a strong Straight. With two cards yet to be turned over. Either an Ace or 9 would do it. The thought of the girls stripping off was made him feel horny, and to through caution to the wind. "I raise two" he announced, throwing in the chips.

Julia had been holding and looking her cards the whole time. Now she looked again at the table. King 'high' she thought. But maybe something would turn up later. She didn't want to chicken out so early. "I call" she announced. "So, I put in, um, two chips."

Mike considered the situation. He knew from playing regular poker with Steve that he had a tendency to over-raise, so despite the table cards not really helping him, with his pair he might as well stay as he was for now and see what turned up. "I call" he echoed, throwing in two more chips.

Thanks to the Flop cards, Ali now had a pair of 10s. She glanced sideways at Steve. She figured he seemed the sort to bluff. "Well", she thought, let's see how strong they think their hands are. "Raise two" she announced, throwing in four chips, to meet Steve's bet and raise it further.

A slight murmur of surprise could be felt at this, but then everyone called, putting in a further two chips each. This betting had already seriously eaten into the starting chip stacks, and there were two more betting rounds to go.

Once Mike had called Ali's bet, she announced "The Turn" and dealt another card into the middle. 8

of hearts.

"Damn", thought Steve. One off the 9 he was hoping for. "I check" he announced.

Julia then Mike both checked also. Ali now had two pairs. Worth another raise she figured. "Raise two".

Steve now had a dilemma; surely, Ali had something, whereas he had nothing unless a 9 or an Ace arrived to save him. But he'd kick himself if he folded now, when one more card could win it for him. "Call" he announced reluctantly, throwing in another two chips. Julia stared at her cards. She could see that she her 9 and 6 went with the 10 and 8 on the table, so one card off a straight. That could be likely, surely? "I call, too" she added, pushing another two chips into the centre.

Mike was now thinking his low pair was looking decidedly average, given how the betting was going. "I fold" he announced. Ali let out a chuckle. "Well Mike, as the first one out, it's down to you to wear the forfeit for the rest of the hand" she advised, pointing to the suspender belt. Steve clapped his hands, laughing. "Well, they are your colours" exclaimed Julia, teasing. "I'm not sure it'll fit, my waist isn't that thin" objected Mike.

"I think you'll find it stretches, and you're not that fat!" commented Ali.

Sure enough, the garment reached around the thinnest part of Mike's waist, to the delight of his three onlookers.

"Huh, reminds me of the time I went to see the Rocky Horror Show, all dressed up!" he reminisced.

"What a sight you must have been" teased Julia.

"Something of a sight now" quipped Steve.

"Since you're out of this hand, can you fetch the white wine from the fridge" requested Ali. "And another bottle of the alcohol-free beer for Steve".

"Sure, no problem" replied Mike, glad to be away from everyone's gaze and comments for a few moments.

They all watched and smirked as Mike wandered into the Kitchen.

Ali called, and then dealt the remaining River card into the centre. 7 of hearts. Julia let out a gasp and her face lit up with a smile. Ali and Steve exchanged knowing glances. Steve folded.

"I can raise a maximum of, um, four?" queried Julia.

"Yes, that's right" replied Ali. "So, you'll need to buy more chips. And that means settling your 'debt' by taking off your skirt, and nominating your next item of clothing."

"Right" confirmed Julia. The hand was now too good not to bet generously, she thought. "OK then, here goes." With that, she unfastened her skirt, unzipped, and eased it down. She had thought she had done so in a not-too revealing manner, shielding herself behind the table, but at just that moment Mike returned from the kitchen. "Nice knickers" he commented, flashing a smile at Julia as he passed behind her, getting an eyeful of lacy black underwear. Julia huffed in mock annoyance, then giggled at the sight of Mike still wearing the belt. "Shall I lend you my stockings as well?" she jibed.

"What clothing item are you nominating now?" enquired Ali, bringing the discussion back to the game.

"Ok, well, I'll go with my blouse I suppose" Julia replied.

"Then here are your next ten chips" responded Ali, counting out the coins from the bank and passing them over. Julia added them to the two chips she had remaining, then pushed four of them into the pot for the bet.

Mike uncorked the wine, and then looked at the glasses; Ali had finished her wine, and Julia then knocked back the remainder of hers. "You don't mind using the same glasses?" he asked. Mike was usually a stickler for not adding white wine into glasses previously used for red, with the liquid mixing and developing a slightly pink tinge. But Ali and Julia didn't seem to care; nodding their heads, only briefly glancing and flashing smiles of encouragement at him, engrossed in the game. So, Mike poured them a full glass of the white wine each. Mike still had a little red wine left himself, and he figured it would be best if he didn't drink any more since he'd be driving later.

"I fold" Ali announced.

"Wow, I win" exclaimed Julia. "Um, do I show my cards, then?"

"Well, you don't need to, because no-one else is left in." explained Ali. "So just pass them all to me"

Ali also prompted Julia to collect the pot of coins; thirty-four in total, adding to her remaining stack of eight, so forty-two in all.

"Are you sure you're a novice at this game?" enquired Steve, humorously, as he helped push the pot chips towards Julia. "With wins like that, we don't stand much chance against you!"

"Well, a lucky start for me, and… hang on, I won, but I'm the only one stripping!" she observed. The others laughed.

"Yes, that's the way it is, but don't worry, everyone else isn't that far behind you" observed Mike.

"Can't I 'buy' back my skirt with all these chips?" questioned Julia.

"No, not in this game!" exclaimed Ali, somewhat forcefully, but matter-of-fact. "Dressing is for when you've stopped playing. For now, your stash of chips needs to be made use of for aiding your position in the game."

"Yeah, so basically don't lose or over-bet, and you won't need to shed any more clothes" added Steve, smiling.

Ali collected all the cards, shuffled them, then passed the pack to Steve along with the dealer token. Steve gave the cards another quick shuffle, and then dealt the second hand. Now it was Julia who put a chip in for the Small Blind, and Mike two for the Big Blind. That meant Mike had two chips remaining.

Ali, with one of the weaker hands in Poker, 8 of hearts and 3 of clubs, immediately folded, then so did Steve, who had the recognised absolute worst hand of 7 Spades and 2 of hearts. Since neither of them were the blinds, that cost them nothing.

Julia looked her hand, comprising 10 hearts and 9 of spades, and encouraged by her initial victory, figured her luck would now continue. "I call" she proclaimed, adding one chip into the pot to match her Small Blind contribution.

Mike looked at his cards, 4 of Diamonds and 3 of spades, and since the other two were already out, he figured he had a chance of this going his way. "I Raise, two" he stated, throwing in his last two chips.

Julia called again, matching Mike's raise with another two chips.

Steve dealt the Flop: King, 8 and 7 of diamonds.

Julia was encouraged by the 10, 9, 8, 7 on offer, meaning she was one off a straight, and so figured she should raise again. "I raise, two" she announced, throwing in two chips.

Mike on the other hand was excited by the four cards of diamonds meaning a flush was one away for him. "Raise two, again" he announced. But in order to do so, he needed more chips. So, he proceeded to remove his jumper in the standard awkward male manner of yanking it up and over his head, revealing his smart checked shirt. "Shirt next time" he pledged. Ali handed him an additional ten chips. Mike and then Julia tossed into the pot two chips each.

Steve then dealt the Turn: 2 of Spades. Not the suit Mike was looking for, or the number for Julia. So, they both checked.

Steve dealt the final River card: Queen of Spades. No good to either of them, leaving both of them with nothing but a King 'high', but with the marginally better hand going to Julia. But Julia, disappointed at not getting the straight, visibly slumped in disappointment, which Mike picked up on. Mike was equally disappointed about not getting a flush, but was a more shewed player; and he was willing to try out a bluff. "Raise four" he announced, throwing in the chips.

Julia has taken aback with surprise. She stared at her cards again and then at the community cards, looking especially at the King and Queen. She had nothing, but Mike could easily have at least of pair, or better. "I fold" she announced. Mike smoothly through his cards away face down, and raked in the pot of twenty chips, with a slender smile on his face.

"What about the forfeit, Mike?" added Ali, giving Mike an expectant look.

"Well, I'll tell you what, I will 'gift' this fetching garment, to you Julia, which should go nicely with your stockings" offered Mike, unclipping the belt.

"Thanks Mike, how generous!" accepted Julia, smiling, taking the belt, and then fastening around her waist and clipping the suspenders to her now exposed stocking tops. "How nice to receive a gift. Twice, in fact" she laughed, meeting Mike's smile, as Ali and Steve nodded in recognition.

The cards were collected, the dealer button moved to Julia, who efficiently dealt out the hand, showing that she had some skill with cards after all.

"The Big Blind raises to four now" announced Ali. So Mike put in two chips for the small blind.

"Time for me to settle my debt and buy-in further" Ali announced, pointing in front of her to indicate she only had two chips left, but needed four for the big blind, and then standing, she reached behind her back and expertly unzipped her dress, then slip it down, slowly enough to ensure she had everyone's attention as she revealed her stunning nude coloured lingerie, beautiful body and magnificent big boobs.

"Well, I will nominate my bra as my next item" she stated, brushing seductively her hands over the cups of her bra, brushing her breasts gently with her fingers. She must have realised that from the look of the men they were getting aroused, and even Julia was enjoying the show. Instead of sitting down immediately, she leaned over the table slightly to retrieve another ten chips from box containing the 'bank', accentuating her cleavage for maximum effect, before taking her seat once again.

Steve managed to pull his gaze from Ali to look his cards. An Ace of hearts and a 5 of clubs. Could be promising, but too early to know. With the stunning view of Ali, Julia sitting on his other side seeming hot with no skirt, and suspenders all round, Steve felt now was not the time to be shy about things, so worth at least hanging in to see how the cards develop.

"Call" he stated, without the confidence he hoped he had. Down to two chips also, he whipped of his sweatshirt, revealing a black T-shirt with a motorcycle image displayed, and a caption reading 'Born to Ride'. "And I guess I'll go for taking my T-shirt off next time" he stated, as Ali passed him another ten chips from the bank. He then put the required four chips into the pot.

Now with everyone having stripped off an item of clothing, the number of chips in circulation had been doubled to eighty.

Julia, her confidence dented by the defeat to Mike, decided to fold since a 6 of hearts and 3 of Diamonds didn't amount to much, and also realising it would cost her nothing.

Mike looked at his cards. The Ace of Spades, and 4 of diamonds. Worth waiting to see if another Ace appears he thought. "Call" he stated, throwing in two chips to add to his Small Blind.

Ali looked at hers. 8 of Spades, and 3 of diamonds. So, nothing worth raising, but as Big Blind, checking cost her nothing more.

Julia dealt the three Flop cards: King of Hearts, 10 of diamonds and 2 of Spades.

Mike, then Ali and Steve all checked. Julia dealt the Turn card: Jack of Diamonds. The three of them all checked again.

Julia then dealt the final River card: 9 of Hearts.

Mike figured with all the checking, no-one had anything. So it was worth him trying another small bluff, since his previous one against Julia had been so successful; his Ace might anyway be enough to win the hand. "Bet four" he announced.

Ali immediately folded. "Good" thought Mike.

Steve looked across the table at Mike; ordinarily, he would fold with not even a pair in his hand, but he also knew Mike would try his luck with a bluff from time-to-time, and suspected that is what he did to Julia. Here he was again probably making a chance raise this late in the hand. "I call" he stated, throwing in four chips to match Mike's bet.

"Bother" thought Mike, who had hoped Steve would fold. "Worth a go anyway" he mused.

They laid their cards down together; everyone stared for a moment, to work out who had won. Mike's Ace, King, 10, 9, 2 was beaten by Steve's Ace, King, 10, 9, 5.

"Only one card in it" exclaimed Steve, in surprise who then chuckled as he raked in the pot of twenty coins.

"So close, indeed" agreed Mike, shrugging his shoulders.

"Do you have an idea for a forfeit, Steve?" questioned Ali.

"Oh, well, um, all I can think of is getting Mike to

down a drink, but I guess you're driving, Mike?"

Mike began to nod in agreement. But then Ali caught his eye.

"Well, you're all welcome to stay here" Ali offered, glancing around the table. "I have plenty of room space."

Mike exchanged looks with Julia.

"Well, if you're sure you don't mind" Julia answered.

"Yes, that would be very nice" agreed Mike

"Ok then, that's settled" confirmed Ali. "Now you can relax, Mike. Since we're nearly out of wine now, how about some Scotch? The bottle and glasses are in that cabinet next to you."

"Sure" acknowledged Mike, who leant across, and opening the cupboard was impressed to find a full bottle of Isle of Jura 12-year aged single malt Scotch Whisky. He fished it out, together with 4 large glass tumblers. He filled one of them with a finger of drink, raised his glass, and promptly drank it down in one. Mike pushed two of the other glasses towards Ali and Julia, and with them both nodding, he poured a measure into his and their glasses, but paused as he looked at Steve.

Steve smiled, watching Mike, then added: "Thanks Ali, that's very kind. I may take you up on that, as long as I don't get called out. If I do, then hopefully any job will be local so I can go and come back." Steve looked at his watch. "But, if I don't hear anything in the next hour, I'm sure I won't be needed anyway."

"Ok, Steve, I understand" replied Ali.

"Let's hope you don't get a call, then" added Julia, smiling at Steve, who held her gaze for a moment.

Now the Button passed to Mike, who dealt the next hand. Ali chipped in two coins for the Small Blind, and Steve four for the Big Blind.

Julia looked at her cards: 8 of spades and 5 of hearts. She wasn't sure this would amount to anything, but felt she couldn't fold twice in a row. Better stick with it for now she thought. "Call" she announced, as she threw in the four chips.

Mike on the other hand, with 5 of clubs and 2 of diamonds, figured that it wasn't even worth the call. "I fold" he stated, throwing his cards in, having contributed nothing.

Ali looked at hers. 7 of diamonds and 5 of spades. She figured it was worth the adding to her Small Blind to stay in for now. "Call" she confirmed, putting two coins into the pot.

Steve looked at his cards. 4 of diamonds and 3 of spades. Could turn into something, he thought. Anyway, he was the Big Blind. He checked.

Mike dealt the Flop cards: Queen of Hearts, 9 of clubs, 6 of spades.

Ali and Steve checked. But Julia saw 9 and 8, 6 and 5; one away from a straight. A small raise is in order she thought. "Raise two" she announced.

"Sorry, but the minimum raise is now four" corrected Ali. "As the Big Blind is now four."

"Oh yes, silly me" replied Julia, slightly embarrassed. "Raise four, then." She counted out the four chips and added them in.

Ali wondered for a minute. She too could see the possibilities for a straight with 9 and 7, 6, 5. "Call" she announced, matching Julia's raise with her last four coins.

Steve didn't think it was worth him staying in any longer. "I fold" he stated, throwing the cards down.

Mike dealt the Turn card: Jack of spades.

That didn't change anything for the girls. Check they both stated.

Mike dealt the final river card: 5 of diamonds. Now they both had a pair of 5s. But only the same community cards. They both checked.

Laying down the cards, they stared for a moment to work out who had won. Then the realisation struck all of them.

"Draw" announced Mike.

"What happens now, then?" queried Julia.

"Well, we split the pot evenly" answered Ali. She counted out and confirmed the split of 10 chips each.

"So, who's forfeit choice is it then?" asked Steve, smiling, who was liking these embellishments to the game.

"Well, no-ones I suppose" replied Ali, slowly, thinking. "I know, Julia and I will both kiss the winner of the next hand!"

"What if one of you is the winner?" queried Mike.

"Well, then we'll both kiss the one with the lowest hand" answered Ali.

"Ok, then" confirmed Julia.

Everyone smirked, thinking of the possibilities.

Now the Button returned to Ali, having done a complete circle of the players.

"The Big Blind raises to eight" she announced, before dealing the cards.

"Now things get serious" remarked Mike.

"Yes, normally this when my luck deserts me" sighed Steve, who had been at the wrong end of big bets from Mike in previous card games.

Steve put in four coins for the Small Blind, and Julia counted out eight for the Big Blind.

Mike looked at his cards. A pair of Aces; Spades and Diamonds. "Fantastic start", he thought.

"Raise eight" Mike confidently announced, but in doing so he had to unbutton and remove his shirt, exposing his shapely and smooth hairless chest. "It's going to be my trousers after this" he confirmed. Ali handed him another ten chips, all of which plus six of his remaining fourteen chips went straight into the pot, leaving him with eight chips and only two items of clothing, having already agreed to the request to ditch his socks.

Ali looked at her hand. A pair of Kings; spades and hearts. No doubt she was certainly in. Just a question of whether to raise even further; she decided to stick with Mike's raise for now. That still meant her having to shed another clothing item too. Slowly Ali reached behind her back, her fingers slightly trembling as they wrestled with the catch, betraying the slight nervousness she felt at this critical moment in the game for her exposing herself. Then it gave way, and her bra popped forward, in a jerk, but not so quickly that she could move her hands around to her front and support it against her breasts. Now she had everyone's attention, even though they tried hard not to be staring. Then one at a time, Ali, lowed the straps down off her shoulders. Then she paused seductively for a moment. In a final movement, she whipped off her bra with one hand, while, covering her breasts with her other arm. Next, she held the bra aloft, gave it a slight wave, and dropped it onto the growing pile of clothing. As she did so, she moved her arms to her sides, and let her ample breasts drop, whilst simultaneously giving them a slight shake from a side-to-side wiggle of her hips, and smiled seductively at the others. Both the boys felt that their mouths had dropped open and frozen, captivated by the sight.

She allowed another moment of pause before shattering the silence by confirming "Call", and throwing in sixteen chips, leaving her with just 4 chips and 2 items of clothing. "It will be my panties next, I shall leave my suspenders and stocking to last" Ali announced, which caused another brief period of stunned reflection.

Steve swigged the rest of his beer to settle himself, then finally examined his cards. With them showing an 8 and 7 of the same suit of diamonds, it seemed promising, though too early to be certain. "Call" he announced, throwing in twelve chips to add to his Small Blind amount of four.

Julia, studied her cards; a pair of 10s; hearts and clubs, which was very good she thought, but would hold off raising further for now.

"Call" she stated, as she put in eight chips, bringing her total to sixteen with her Big Blind.

Ali then dealt the three Flop cards: King of Clubs, and the 10 and 9 of Diamonds.

"Excellent" thought Ali, and Steve was encouraged too, both of them trying to maintain their poker faces. "How wonderful" Julia was thinking, and she beamed a broad smile. Mike tried not to be concerned.

It was Steve's turn to start the betting again; he was one off a flush or a Straight, or both, but he couldn't consider raising yet. "Check" he announced, not adding to the pot. Julia followed with a check too, her three of a kind seeming strong to her, but wasn't confident enough to raise things further. Mike also checked, his Pair of Aces not helped by the community cards, but still worth hanging in for now.

Ali, with three of a kind in Kings, wondered about upping the stakes. But that would mean losing another item of clothing, so soon after the previous one. She didn't mind the stripping but didn't want to get too far head of the others. Such is the strange thing about Strip Poker, that loss of clothing can influence bet decisions. So instead, she checked, and then dealt the Turn card into the centre: Jack of clubs.

"Wow", thought Steve, and couldn't contain his smile. A straight, with still the possibility of a flush or even a straight flush with the last card, he thought.

"Raise eight" he stated. Now he had to take off his T-shirt, throwing it onto the pile, revealing his muscular looking hairy chest. "It's my jeans next" he stated, as Ali passed him 10 more coins, then he put in eight more coins to leave him with six remaining, and two items of clothes.

Julia considered her cards; three of a kind in 10s seemed excellent to her. But Steve has just raised, so maybe that was enough for now she thought. "I call" she announced, throwing in another eight chips to match Steve's raise.

Mike looked at his cards and wondered what everyone else had. Although a pair of Aces was an excellent start, it seemed to him that at least one person must have something strong with all the raises. But he was one off a Royal Straight, if only a Queen would show up on the last card. It was a risk, as otherwise he was unlikely to have the strongest hand, but reluctantly he knew he had to stay in to find out.

"Call" he announced, throwing in the eight chips and wiping out his funds, with just his two items of clothing remaining.

Ali couldn't drop out now, so she had to face it that she would be down to her final clothing item. "Call" she announced, followed by slowly slipping her knickers down her thighs, over her knees and letting them slide down to her feet. She managed the manoeuvre including getting them off her feet, into her hand and onto the clothing pile whilst hiding her lower half behind the table. Not that she was leaving much to the imagination now. "Just my stockings and suspenders to go" she announced, to the only-just suppressed excitement of all. Providing herself with her final ten chips, Ali added eight into the extensive pot, with just 6 chips left. Then Ali dealt the final River card: Jack of hearts.

They all did a double-take, taking in the realisation. There was a sharp intake of breath from Steve.

He had missed out a straight flush, just the wrong suit of Jack, twice! But surely, he thought, a regular straight was still enough to win? "Raise eight" he announced. Then he stood up, undid his belt and pulled his jeans down, to display his Marks & Spencer mid blue spotted boxer shorts. He yanked his jeans down, bending over to pull them off his bare feet; like Mike he had already discarded his socks. Then he took his place back at the table, Ali having pushed his last ten chips to his spot, so he could throw eight into the pot, leaving him with eight remaining.

Julia on the other hand had a Full house; three 10s and two Jacks. She had no hesitation. "Raise eight" she stated.

To be able to match Steve's raise and afford her

own, she also needed to remove a clothing item. So, she unbuttoned and removed her flowery blouse to reveal a lacy black bra which matched her knickers, her remaining two items of clothing, not counting her stockings and suspenders which she had retained but had agreed wouldn't count towards the game's betting. She nominated the bra as the next item to be removed, her last-but-one piece of clothing, as Ali passed her ten coins. Once she had added the required sixteen to the pot, she was left with six coins.

Although he now had two pairs thanks to the community cards, Mike felt his hand didn't seem strong enough to stay in, given the way the betting was now going. "I fold" stated Mike, throwing in his cards.

It was all-or-nothing time for Ali. Her Full House of three Kings and two Jacks was such a strong hand that it had to be worth taking the gamble head-on.

"All in" Ali announced, pushing her remaining six chips into the pot. "Everything I have is now in, but don't let that stop you continuing to bet" she remarked to Julia.

"Oh, so what happens if I bet more than you then?" Julia asked, intrigued.

"Then we create a 'side pot' which only those who have added more can win" explained Ali.

Steve then called, adding his last eight chips, also going All-in, which concluded the betting.

They laid their cards down. Ali had the strongest hand, her three Kings bettering Julia's three 10s, with both of the having the two Jacks.

"Two Full Houses" gasped Mike.

"I thought my straight would be enough" complained Steve.

"Goodness, and I thought my Full House was a sure winner" added Julia.

Ali beamed, and collected the main pot of 114 chips. Julia, to her surprise and mild delight, gained 20 chips from the side pot since Ali hadn't matched the last bet.

"I could have won, if only that last card had been the Jack of Hearts", observed Steve. "Then I would have had a straight flush!"

Out of chips and so needing to shed his final item of clothes, Steve added "Well, that's me out of the game, then". He stood up, and swiftly and confidently yanked down his boxers, to reveal his dark public hair surrounding his semi-flaccid penis.

"Ah, but now it's time for the promised forfeit" reminded Ali.

At that, she rose from her chair, and looking at Julia, encouraged her with the slightest gesture of her hand to do likewise. They shuffled around Steve, who, realising what was going on, stood up to face them. The girls moved slowly together ever closer to Steve, until all their lips almost touched. But Ali put her hand on Julia's shoulder, and pressed gently downwards. She instinctively understood, and together they both sank to their knees. Steve's dick, from its previously resting state, now sprung to attention. Ali and Julia's lips touched each other as they came together at his cock. They kissed as one, rolling their tongues around his bellend, causing Steve's erection to stiffen, while their lips touched each other as well. Then they withdrew slightly, still shoulder-to-shoulder, and stood up to raise their mouths to his, where finally their three lips now met, and kissed sensually. Ali then backed away, but Julia moved her mouth to Steve's ear, and whispered provocatively: "I want you to give me a cumshot." As she said this, her hand reached to his groin and her fingers brushed over his balls and then his member, stiffening it even further.

Then she sank to her knees again, and jerked his cock in a rhythmic motion. He looked down at her as she looked up at him, smiling, lips parted. Almost immediately a wave of unstoppable pleasure washed over him as he came, shooting his spunk straight into her mouth, also around her cheeks and she squinted to minimise the splash into her eyes. He then sank to the floor to embrace her, as they kissed briefly but deeply.

Meanwhile, Ali had fetched a box of tissues, and handing them to Julia, who commenced drying her face. Ali then turned to Mike. "Another glass of Scotch is in order I think."

Mike was stunned by what he had just witnessed. Amazed by Ali and Julia's kisses and turned on by the whole sexiness. And a little jealous of Steve, though also pleased for his friend that he saw some 'action'.

Mike recovered his composure, and topped up Ali and Julia glasses, then his, and had very nearly begun to utter the questioning words to Steve as to whether it was late enough that he could now join them for a drink, when at that exact moment, Steve's phone rang. They all paused for an instant, frozen by the intrusive sound.

Steve muttered in exasperation: "What timing, I know exactly who this will be." Sure enough, the unmistakable sound of the BES helpdesk clicked through as soon as he pressed the answer button. The call was urgent and brief, with Steve nodding and agreeing before hanging up with the parting words "… so you'll text me the exact site details and situation report."

Steve, seemingly to have forgotten that he was standing naked in the middle of the room having just ejaculated into Julia's still slightly moist face, glanced around to the other three, sporting an expression of annoyance. "Typical, I have to go, just when I was enjoying myself for once!"

After Steve had hurriedly dressed, said his thanks and gave his apologises to Ali, and promised that if he could, would be back to join them all somewhat much later, he shot away on his motorcycle. The others urged him to be careful.

Mike shook his head in dismay when he learnt where the helpdesk was sending him.

"Marlborough! That is going to take forever!" he exclaimed.

Steve tried to play it down. "On the bike I can get there quickly, probably the generator just needs restarting, and I'll be back before you know it" he claimed, though he knew in reality it would be at least an hour each way, and could be in for a long haul once he got there to sort out the site issues.

Julia gave him a long farewell kiss. "Take care, I'll be waiting for your return, so we can carry on where we left off" she whispered in his ear.

Once Steve had left, the others grouped around the table again to complete the game. With Steve out, the dealing passed to Julia. Mike had to put in for the

Small Blind, but out of coins, he stripped off his trousers to reveal his skimpy Calvin Klein underpants, black but with a white waist band. Ali handed him his final ten coins, which reduced to six with four going into the pot. Ali put eight in for the Big Blind. Then Julia looked at her cards. Ace and 4 of clubs. Ever the optimist, Julia called, counting into the pot eight coins.

Mike looked at his hand. Ace of Spades and 3 of hearts. He couldn't see much else to do than staying in, especially since half the bet was already made with his Small Blind, so he called, adding 4 coins. Ali had 9 and 6 of hearts, and as the Big Blind just checked, completing the round, so Julia dealt the Flop: Ace of hearts, 5 of diamonds and 4 of spades. Mike was pleased with his pair of Aces, but tried not to show it. It was him to start the betting. With only two coins left, he figured he should proceed with caution. "Check" he announced. Ali checked, and Julia, with her two pairs of Aces and fours was delighted, but checked too, much to Mike's relief. Julia dealt the Turn: 3 of hearts. That gave Mike a double pair, but he didn't feel he needed to bet his last coins yet. He checked, as did both of the girls in turn. Julia dealt the final River card: 2 of Spades.

"Bingo" thought Mike, just what he had been hoping for. Now his hand was transformed into a Straight, giving him the confidence bet what little he had left.

"All-In" Mike announced, adding his remaining 2 coins.

Little did he know, that Ali had picked up what she needed to make a Straight too. "Raise eight" she stated, pilling in ten chips to match Mike's raise and for her own. Julia did a double take, delighted in realising she also had a Straight and, regardless of the betting from the others, she figured she was the one with the winning hand. "Raise eight more" she confidently announced, but with a slight giggle, as she was now out of chips. So, she reached behind her back, and unclipped her bra, letting it slide down to reveal her modest but beautifully shaped breasts. Ali slid her final ten coins to her, and she pushed eight into the pot.

Ali had no hesitation in betting a further eight, forcing Julia to go All-in with her remaining two chips.

They laid their cards down. Mike looked at Julia's first, a wry smile appeared on his face as he realised, they had drawn. But then he glanced over at Ali's, and saw that actually they both had been beaten by a higher Straight. "Well played" he managed to say, without sounding disappointed. Ali beamed at her victory, then smirked. "Time to lose your clothes you two, and then one last forfeit" she remarked. "And these two cards give the perfect idea". She pointed to her hand, containing the 6 and 9 of hearts.

Mike duly stripped off his pants, now completely naked. Julia removed her thong, but was still wearing the gifted suspender belt and her stockings. Ali, also still wearing her suspender belt and stockings, beckoned them into the corridor off the living room, and into through the first door. Inside was a spacious bedroom with a king size double bed.

"Lay down, Mike" she instructed. Mike lay face up, his anticipated pleasure indicated by his growing erection. Ali gestured, but she didn't need to as Julia understood and was more than willing. She climbed on the bed and then straddled Mike, 'head-to-tail', and brought her body down on his. As her mouth took in Mike's penis and her parted lips closed around the tip, her bottom sank towards Mike's face, allowing his tongue to lick her pussy. Sensually they kissed and caressed each other's genitals, both becoming more and more aroused. Ali sat on the corner of the bed and watched with growing excitement until she could no longer resist and end her lack of involvement. She climbed over the bed and her hands gently pulled Julia's head up and guided her body to sit upright, with Mike's face still in position. As Julia moved, Ali closed in, swinging her leg over to straddle Mike's lower body, guiding his erect member into her vagina, now fully hard and lubricated with Julia's warm saliva. Finally, the rearrangement of their bodies was complete and the threesome engaged as Ali's mouth and tongue met Julia's and they passionately kissed, with their arms wrapped around and caressing each other. Mike's arms reached up and his hands found Ali's cracking boobs as he continued to lick and suck Julia's parts. Ali began thrusting herself up and down on Mike's cock; he did his best to delay the inevitable, but with the rhythm being controlled by Ali there wasn't much he could do to prolong the moment very long. As his semen exploded up and inside Ali, she orgasmed too, her vagina pulsing around Mike's cock, adding to his pleasure. Julia could sense their enjoyment which turned her on more, so she guided one of Mike's hands to her clitoris. The combination of the lick of his tongue and the touch of his fingers, together with Ali massaging her breasts, rapidly sent her over the edge too.

The girls rolled off Mike's body and the three of

them spread out in the luxuriously large bed, the duvet for which had been folded at the end, but Ali managed to yank a corner of it up and the others pulled it up and over them to envelope their three bodies. Next, the girls removed the suspender belts and peeled off their stockings. With them all naked now, they continued to enjoy the caress each other's hands and mouths for some time. Eventually, together they drifted off into a sound and satisfying deep sleep.

7 CALL-OUT

Steve thumbed the electric starter on his Honda motorcycle, and the engine roared into life. He pulled in the clutch lever, pressed down the gear level into first gear, and then smoothly released clutch as he wound open the throttle twist-grip, moving swiftly away from Ali's house. The evening had been beyond his wildest dreams, and part of him was wondering why he hadn't made up some excuse saying he couldn't make the call-out, instead of loyally following instructions from his employer that he had already lost his love for. Just too dedicated and task-oriented he supposed.

Although Marlborough was hardly close-by, fortunately he knew the small market town well and was confident of reaching the BCS site swiftly, without confusion, knowing that it was located to the south, on the edge of Savernake Forest. It didn't take him long to leave the Bristol area and join the M4 motorway at junction 19. Twisting his right wrist to open up the throttle, rapidly changing up the gears with his right foot and in perfect synchronisation with his left hand engaging the clutch he accelerated hard. He felt the wind whistle past his helmet and was pleased of his leather jacket, gloves and trousers keeping his warm from the chill of the cool night air. He changed up into the top gear of sixth, and then cruised at just beyond 70 mph speed limit. The CB500 he was riding was capable of doing a bit more than a 'ton' but he was sensible enough not to go too fast and risk being pulled over by the police, or probably more likely being flashed by a speed camera. In just over half-an-hour, he saw the sign for the Junction 16, the first Swindon turning. The main road to Marlborough is at the one beyond, but Steve knew an alternative back route that would suit him and the bike better. Exiting the motorway and picking up the B4005 minor road from the roundabout, he found Hay Lane and the road to Broad Hinton. From there he hung a left turn on the road that would have led to the Neolithic stone circle at Avebury and instead swept past the iconic Hackpen White horse chalk hill figure, and kept going until he arrived at the outskirts of Marlborough, via Free's Avenue, and into Kingsbury Street. Joining the London Road, he pottered through the centre of the town, past the characterful old buildings and shops that lined the wide high street of this vibrant market town. Traffic was relatively light at this time of night, though there was quite a bustle of people on foot out enjoying the pubs and restaurants. Steve smiled in recognition as he rode past the Red Lion, where he had once met the famous TV 'Doctor Who' actor Tom Baker at an artist's exhibition. For some reason had taken a shine to his motorcycle and had been very complementary. They had chatted for a few pleasant moments but he now shook his head in mild regret that he had been so taken aback that hadn't asked for an autograph or selfie.

Exiting the town, he got onto the A4 towards Savernake Forest, and as he past the hospital, he spotted the BES sign pointing toward the site location. “Easy” thought Steve, figuring that his journey had taken less than the expected hour. “Maybe this will be a simple job” he mused to himself. Steve parked his bike at the gated entrance and getting off, was even more heartened to see a familiar looking purple coloured pick-up following up behind him down the access road. Sure enough, it parked behind him and the occupant got out; recognition was instant.

“Mr. Martin, how the devil are you?” enquired the new arrival.

“Mr. Smith, how good of you to join me” Steve jested in reply.

“Well, someone had to bring the tools, instead of just showing off on their ‘silver dream racer’” the reply came.

The men had known each other for some years, and worked well together. Both shared an ironic sense of humour, but were fiercely loyal; they knew they could depend on each other. And they shared something else, too: they were both called Steve!

“So, what do we have here, then” asked Steve S as an introduction.

“Well, I’m sure I don’t know, having only got here a minute ago” replied Steve M. “But most likely we’ll just have to restart the generator and all will be well, for a few days at least, I would hope”

The men gained access to the site and started running through the troubleshooting diagnosis. As predicted by Steve M, the generator was displaying various alarms and not functioning, causing other electrical equipment to fail. Following the restart procedures brought everything back online.

"Well, seems like we might away from here in no time after all" pronounced Steve M, more to himself than to Steve S. It was at that moment they heard a scraping noise, and turned just in time to watch his motorcycle slide off its side-stand, which had been positioned in a rush by Steve at an unfortunate angle, and crash onto the floor.

"Bother the thing!" cried out Steve M. "I'll go and pick it up and move it"

"Sure, no worries, I'll just finish off here while you do that and then we'll be nearly done" replied Steve S, concerning himself with the equipment.

Steve M marched back to his Bike, pulled it up off the floor, and propped it up against himself. He considered on closer inspection that the ground where he had positioned it, to one side of the gate to allow Steve S access with his vehicle, to be unsuitably soft and sloping. So, donning his helmet, he began to manoeuvre it around to face back towards the way in, so he could ride it up the track to firmer ground. Suddenly, there was the most ear-splitting sound of an explosion, followed by a fireball accompanied by wave of pressure that knocked Steve off his feet, him and his bike rolling onto the ground. Within moments, everything seemed to be engulfed in flames and smoke.

8 ACCIDENT

Mike was awoken by his mobile phone ringing. He groggily reached out for it, and tried to focus; he couldn't quite believe the time and the caller. He recognised immediately it was from the BES helpdesk, but it was a surprise for him to be receiving a call from them at 6am on a Saturday morning.

"Hello?" answered Mike

"This is Ryan from the BES helpdesk. Is that Mike Richards?" the caller asked.

"Yes, this is he."

"You are a nominated Emergency contact for Steve Martin; we haven't been able to reach anyone else from his other contacts."

"Not surprising at 6am on a Saturday" mused Mike, more to himself.

"Yes, sorry about this early call, but we wanted to advise that regrettably he has been involved in an accident …"

Once the call ended, Mike hurriedly started getting dressed, while updating the girls who were now wide awake. Julia got dressed quickly too, while Ali had flung a robe on, and disappeared into the Kitchen. Julia grabbed her handbag and nipped in the bathroom to do a rapid job on her make-up. Meanwhile Ali returned with two travel mugs of steaming coffee, and a pair of small blueberry muffins.

"Clearly you don't have time for breakfast, so this will have to do to send you on your way" remarked Ali.

"Wow, thanks" replied Mike, who was wide awake now and the smell of the coffee was divine.

They embraced and shared a long, lingering kiss.

"Go now. See your friend is o.k." Ali spoke softly in his ear. "Return when you can."

"Yes, I will. I'll be back to see you soon" promised Mike.

Julia emerged from the bathroom, looking beautifully presentable in contrast to Mike's stubbly unkempt appearance. Ali ran her hand across his hair in a vain attempt at smartening him up slightly.

Julia thanked Ali, who winked back at her.

"Wow" she exclaimed at the sight of the drinks and snacks.

Final hurried embraces, then they were rushing out the door, and roaring away in Mike's BMW.

"I can drop you off at yours" suggested Mike.

"No way, I need to see Steve's alright. I'm coming with you to … Marlborough, is it?"

"No, there's no A&E facility at the local hospital, he's been taken to the Great Western at Swindon. I know that well as that's where my sister works. Mmm, that's a thought" Mike mused.

Speed dialling his mobile with his car's hands-free Bluetooth system, he got straight though to Helen's voicemail. He left a bit of a garbled message, which he hoped she'd understand. A few minutes later,

Helen rang him back.

"My goodness, Mike, you're sure it was your 'best man' Steve in the accident? Horrific fire or explosion in Marlborough I understand …" began Helen, in her no-nonsense way.

Mike had forgotten Helen and Steve had met at his Wedding. At one stage Mike had even wondered if they might hit it off, though Steve was always too reserved and Helen was so direct she wouldn't stand shy and retiring.

"…anyway, as I recall, man with third-degree burns, not in great shape. But I'll have to check" added Helen.

Julia gasped a cry of alarm, which Helen picked up on.

"Someone with you Mike?"

"Sorry, yes, I have Julia in the car, she's …" Mike began to explain.

"Steve's girlfriend" added Julia, to Mike's surprise.

"Oh, hello; sorry it's not good news. But I need to find out more, so try not to worry. I've got to go now, when you arrive, find me and I'll update you and try to speed you through.

There was a nervous silence between them for the rest of the journey along the M4 motorway. The tension was only broken by Julia feeding Mike bits of his muffin as he drove. She didn't feel like eating herself at first, but then started nibbling to stop herself biting her nails. Eventually, Mike was relieved to see the sign for Junction 15, where he turned off and followed the signs to the Great Western hospital. As typical, the car park looked very full, so Mike dropped Julia off at the entrance and went to hunt down a parking space. Add he did so, his phone rang. It was Joy. "Bother", thought Mike; he should have called her before now.

"Hi, love" greeted Mike.

"I thought you might have rung me last night or at least this morning by now, since we're always up early, to see how Thomas and I are getting along" replied Joy. "But I guess you probably had too many beers with Steve last night."

Mike launched into a description of Steve's call-out and accident, explaining he was now in Swindon to find out more, which had an understandable shocking effect on Joy, promptly forgetting about Mike's lack of communication. They chatted for a short time, while Mike manoeuvred his car up and down hunting out a space.

"Let me know what the situation is when you can, later" Joy requested.

"Will do" Mike promised, as he finally located a parking place and slid the BMW into it. He dashed into the hospital, and spotted Julia at the desk. As she saw him, she motioned in the direction of the Urgent Treatment Centre (UTC) towards the West Entrance, where the Emergency Department (ED) is located.

"I understand only one person can visit at once" Julia explained, looking glum.

"Ok, well, let's see what they say" replied Mike.

At the UTC, Mike asked about Steve, speaking to a clinical navigator, who looked concerned as she examined the records.

"Steve … Smith?" she muttered to herself.

Mike and Julia were confused.

"I think Steve Smith has his mum with him right now" came a voice from behind them.

There was a tap on Mike's shoulder. He and Julia spun around.

Helen and Steve Martin stood there, smiling.

"Found this one safe, and almost sound!" announced Helen.

Mike burst into laughter in relief, as Julia dashed over to Steve, hugging him, then giving him a deep kiss.

"Not great news about Steve Smith though" added Steve, grimly, once Julia had released him.

They thanked Helen as she had to rush off to attend other matters. Then the three of them went back to Mike's car, and Steve updated them on the way home.

The generator explosion knocked Steve over and his bike had fallen on top of him. He managed to struggle free and get away, fortunately protected by his helmet and leathers. But his colleague had not been so lucky, having been caught in the fire. Steve had just managed to ring the emergency services and then the BES helpdesk too before his phone died. Steve was worried the petrol tank on his bike or Steve Smith's pickup might explode too. The fire crew and an ambulance were on the scene quickly, and once Steve Smith had been extracted from the site, Steve Martin rode with him in the ambulance.

At the hospital, Steve Smith had been rushed off into the ED, while Steve Martin waited for a long time to be assessed himself. He had been suffering from shock and minor cuts and bruises from the initial blast and from his motorcycle crushing him. He had stayed at the hospital to await Steve Smith's fate, and met his colleague's mum when she arrived. Then he was pleased that Helen had come across him, who he'd chatted to before being reunited with Mike and Julia.

"So my bike's write-off for sure" concluded Steve.

"The sign of a true biker, more worried about his machine than himself" Mike wryly observed.

They arrived at Julia's flat.

"Come in and rest with me for awhile" she requested of Steve. "You shouldn't be alone; I'll take you home afterwards."

Steve followed her out of Mike's car, thanking Mike, who gave him the thumbs up.

Once inside her flat, Julia and Steve kissed, caressing each other's hair and shoulders. Then Julia broke off.

"Given the night and morning you've had, you need some pampering" she commanded. "I shall run a bath for you, with plenty of bubbles." That she did, while Steve pulled off his clothes. He was glad to be shot of his bike leathers, which he dropped by the front door, but his other clothes felt messy, sweaty and uncomfortable having been in them all night. So not surprising that Julia wanted him to spruce up he thought. He also felt rather shattered from the physical exertions as well as having a slightly spaced-out feeling that no sleep had left him with.

Julia invited him into the bathroom, and left him to sink into the beautiful warm soapy water. An instant later, she reappeared, a stunning sight completely naked. She climbed into the bath facing Steve, and lowered herself gently on top of him. Her wonderfully smooth skin and perfect breasts slid effortlessly against his body, and despite his tiredness he was instantly turned on. They kissed, deeply and passionately.

"Maybe I didn't survive that accident" Steve remarked, Steve, looking serious for a brief moment, before breaking into a broad smile. "I must have died and gone to heaven." Julia smiled sweetly at this funny guy. They kissed and caressed some more, before climbing out of the bath and drying on Julia's soft white towels. Naked, Julia took Steve by the hand and led him to her bedroom. It was small but immaculately furnished. Julia gently manoeuvred the uncertain man onto the bed and onto his back. Julia reached into her side table draw and pulled a packet, which she quickly ripped open, and extracted the contents. Holding the teat, she rolled the slippery pink condom down Steve's now very erect penis. Then Julia spread her legs wide and mounted his dick, sliding it inside her to their joint pleasure. Steve reached up and alternated his hands between her arms and her breasts and she rhythmically and increasingly rapidly rode up and down on his cock. Steve didn't think he could contain himself long, but Julia cried out in pleasure as she came, and an instant later Steve complete let go and shot his load, each jerk of his ejaculation sending waves of erotic sensation through both of their bodies. They kissed briefly, then Julia extracted herself from Steve's dick, and Steve slid the now bulging condom off and tied a knot in it to contain the contents, and then climbed up to put it in a bin. Julia intercepted him with a tissue, which she used to collect the sticky sheath, and gave him another to wipe himself while she disposed of it. Then they both climbed back into bed and hugged and kissed some more before drifting off into a well-deserved sound sleep.

A couple of hours later they were up again; Julia slipped on a dress and through a pair of clean boxer shorts at him.

"These should fit you" she advised, and then dug out a plain shirt T-shirt also of his size. Steve wasn't about to ask why she had these items of men's clothing in her cupboards, but the thought briefly crossed his mind that they certainly weren't Mike's, since the shorts were too big and he knew boxer shorts were not to his taste. But as if reading his mind, Julia advised: "My brother Jack's; he's about your build. Handy that he stays here occasionally and leaves me some of his things to wash, the cheeky devil" Julia explained, rolling her eyes and shrugging in mild annoyance. "Ah, and look, a pair of jeans too". Steve was delighted not to need to put yesterday's closes back on; these clothes would suit him fine for now. "Thanks, Jack" he replied in jest. "I'll take good care of these."

"But it's ok, you leave yours here, and I don't mind washing them", she announced, drawing closer to him again, then giving him an affectionate, short kiss. "It might prove handy to keep a change of clothes here. And I'll make sure Jack doesn't borrow them. Luckily, he doesn't like bikes!" she concluded humorously, pointing to the design of Steve's shirt.

"That sounds a perfect arrangement to me, thank you" replied Steve, kissing her back in agreement. "Jack can have these back soon enough" he concluded, tugging at his shirt.

They wandered into the Kitchen and Julia glanced at the wall-clock.

"Time for a quick spot of lunch. I can do, mmm, cheese on toast" Julia announced. Then, catching and holding his gaze for a long moment, and seriously searching his expression, asked: "With Marmite, of course!?"

"Love it!" Steve replied with complete honesty. "You know, I could very much warm to you" he announced, jesting again but still indicating their truly and rapidly growing attraction. Much later, Steve got taken back to his flat by Julia, and they promised they would be seeing each other again very soon.

Meanwhile, Mike had driven away from Julia's flat, mulling over this rapid chain of events. After a such a dreadful night, Mike was delighted that not only Steve was safe, but that he and Julia were now clearly developing a promising relationship; he was pleased for his friend. His thoughts then instantly then turned to Ali. After yesterday's amazing night, he had to see her again. "Just to update her that Steve's ok" he told himself, as he headed towards her cottage. But he knew in his heart he was hoping for much more. And wasn't disappointed when Ali welcomed him in!

"I was so worried" Ali began.

"It's all worked out ok, well, apart from Mr. Smith who's in a critical condition" Mike added, seriously. "But Julia is, err, taking good care Steve who'll be fine I think when he's had some proper rest."

"You need to unwind too, Mike" replied Ali. "Come, take a shower" she offered.

Mike gladly stripped off and got into the big, walk-in shower. And he was even more pleased when Ali, who had been still in her robe, slipped it off and joined him. They slowly and sensuously embraced, caressed and kissed each as the water and shower gel mingled with their naked bodies.

Finally, they exited the shower, dried themselves and entered the bedroom. Climbing on the bed together, they kissed and caressed some more. Then they fucked every which way. Mike particularly liked their first shag doggy-style; as he shot his load into her beautifully erotic warm body they laughed with ecstasy and joy. Then Ali mounted him on top, which clearly she enjoyed immensely, he could now see the attraction of a large breasts, as they bounced provocatively in his face. When they turned over again to adopt the missionary position, Mike couldn't see how things could feel any better when he put his dick between Ali's breasts for a tit-wank; so soft and welcoming, he finished with his cum shooting all over her chest.

Eventually, Mike returned to his house. He was expecting Joy back shortly, and then a thought struck him. He hurried to their bedroom, greeted as expected to a perfectly made unslept-in bed. So, he pulled back the duvet and messed up the sheets and pillows a little. He didn't want to have to explain why he hadn't come home last night.

Steve Smith died of his severe burn injuries in hospital. His funeral was held locally soon afterwards, and attended by many of his BES colleagues, including Julia, Steve Martin and Mike, all naturally dressed in black. Following the church service, they stood in the grounds as the burial took place, and then wandered back to their cars.

"This of course is it for me and BES now" Steve informed Mike. "I've secured a position at Telecom services, starting next month". Mike nodded at the news.

"I'm off too, to that marketing agency in London I mentioned" added Julia. "It will be a good fit, and a mixture of commuting and working from home will suit me fine." She took Steve's hand and squeezed it. Steve, almost blushing then announced "We're looking at sharing a house in or around Reading."

Mike raised his eyebrows, before smiling. "Good for you two" he congratulated.

"What are you going to do, Mike?" asked Steve.

"Well, it's not completely sorted yet, and I'm not supposed to say anything" began Mike, in a lowered voice. But it seems certain now that McConnochie, the Scottish construction group I have been speaking with, is going to take over BES. And they'll want me to manage the business transition. It'll mean I'll be back and forth between Bristol and Glasgow for some time, certainly initially. But then will probably be able to work from home for some of the time."

"I'm sure Joy will be less than delighted by that arrangement" observed Steve. "Where will you live?"

"Yes, that's a good question" replied Mike, shrugging his shoulders. He knew handling the impact on his personal life would be more difficult than undertaking the new business position. "Joy's talking about Knutsford."

Steve and Julia exchanged puzzled looks.

"A nice market town about half way, and not very far from her mum."

Mike watched Steve and Julia drive off together. Then he turned, and as he had expected, saw a familiar figure approaching.

"Hi Mike, how did it go?" asked Ali. "I watched

from a distance, but didn't want to intrude."

"Yeah, ok, obviously sad" replied Mike. "But I'm pleased to see you though."

They kissed, then walked slowly away, hand-in-hand, chatting.

"Did you tell them about Glasgow?" she asked

"Uh-Huh" uttered Mike, his body language pointing to the mixed emotions he had.

"I know it's a big change, but it will be an adventure, for both of us!" enthused Ali. "I'm looking to opening a new shop up there, which will be wonderful. I have so many new ideas."

"Yes, I can see that" replied Mike. "It's just that it's going to take so much time. The BES business migration could take a year, which will mean a lot of back-and-forth. Never mind the ... personal changes. It's frustrating, but I need to get everything sorted."

They stopped walking, and Ali reached in towards and kissed Mike again.

"Don't worry, be bold! It will all work out if you embrace the future. And we have so much time ahead."

9 UP AND AWAY

For Joy's birthday, she and Mike were going hot-air ballooning. Mike had booked it some time ago, as something a bit different to try. He got the sense that Joy wasn't too keen on the idea when he surprised her with it, and now the day had come, he no longer was as enthusiastic either. He'd rather be spending the time with Ali if he could. Plus, Joy had seemed out of sorts the last few days. But it was too late to cancel now. Joy's Mum had taken Thomas to look after him for the day, and they were all set for the experience.

They arrived at the Bristol 'launch site' in good time. The site of the basket sitting there, with the canopy stretched across the field made the idea suddenly very 'real', which excited Mike as someone who embraced 'action' activities, but Joy was clearly looking nervous.

They wandered over to the staff, who checked their names on their register of attendees, and then they went to wait with other couples who were making the flight.

Soon the staff had the balloon inflated, and they were all issued with 'Dream Tours' baseball caps, with the explanation that head protection was advised to avoid your head being uncomfortably heated by the balloon's burner.

Then they were shepherded towards the basket, and encouraged to climb onboard. No sooner and they all done so, then the balloon began to lift slightly, with the sound of the burner now loud as it began heating the air. The restraining ropes were detached, and without delay the balloon took off at what felt like a tremendous speed.

The air whooshed as they rose, together with the burner still making a big noise, but then it was quickly shut off, the air became still and all was dramatically quiet all of a sudden. Now they could enjoy the serene and calm ride.

"What a fantastic view" exclaimed Joy, who's nerves had been replaced by awe at the pleasurable feeling of gently floating.

"I told you it would be great" replied Mike, who's mood had also lifted now they had finally begun the airborne adventure.

They marvelled at the sight of wild animals running about below them, mostly deer and rabbits being startled by their presence, especially when the burner was periodically switched on to maintain their height. Then, looking in the distance, Mike saw a familiar landmark.

"Look, there's Clifton Suspension Bridge" he exclaimed. "I'll miss the sight of that when we move up North.

"Silly, they'll be plenty of bridges and whatnot to look at elsewhere" replied Joy. "And anyway, you'll be continuing to drop down this way quite frequently by the sounds of it, even once we've moved."

The weather was perfect for their trip, but before

too long, it was time to descend, and it was at that point that they realised that this would be the most thrilling, as Mike saw it, or as Joy did, alarming, part of the adventure. As the balloon got lower and lower, the ground seemed to rise up at them, and their speed became much more noticeable, rushing along ground. They were all told to brace for landing, and then the balloon basket deliberately caught a hedge, which caused it top to tip on its side to the gasps of its passengers. But in an instant the basket had landed with a bump, and they were all clambering out over the basket's edge.

"Wow, what a blast!" exclaimed Mike. Joy was silent as she caught her breath, but the broad smile that broke out on her face showed she had enjoyed the experience, or at least pleased to have survived it.

They then had to wait for the Land Rover to locate the field they were in, to ferry them back to where they had parked at the launch site. Meanwhile, the Dream Tours staff had dragged out a wicker hamper and, unpacking it, produced some champagne, orange juice and plastic flutes, as well as A4 certificates commemorating the trip.

The drinks were poured, Mike gratefully receiving the champagne, before noticing Joy had opted for just Orange Juice. They touched their 'glasses' in celebration.

"Now I have some news; we're having another baby" announced Joy, beaming. As Mike looked dumbfounded, she added unnecessarily: "I'm pregnant. I didn't want to say anything until we had completed our flight, otherwise you and especially Mum would have worried so. Fantastic, huh?"

"Yes … of course" uttered Mike, before hugging

and kissing his wife. But inside, his thoughts were raging as he tried to make sense of how things would now unfold.

Ali was in her flat, in a pensive mood. She had just gone to the toilet, and now was looking at the plastic stick in her hand. She stared at the little results window, waiting to see if a line would appear. She knew that the result could mean a dramatic and significant shift in her life, changing everything. As she waited the few minutes it took, in her heart she felt she already knew the outcome, and what it was going to mean for the future.

10 EPILOGUE: NEW BEGINNINGS

Mike reversed his Tanzanite Blue metallic BMW 3 series touring into a familiar parking space; it has been over a year since he had first been visiting this location. As he stopped, the familiar clang that sounded from his bicycle reminded him exactly where he was and why he was here now. He got out, locked the car up with his key fob remote, and strode towards and into the entrance of the service area building. According to habit, he glanced at his watch as he walked. He figured on finding something to purchase and still arrive on time for his planned rendezvous.

As he had anticipated, next to the original boutique shop he knew so well, in the adjacent unit was now another store: "The Looking Glass"; he smiled at the deliberate knowing humour of the choice of name. Inside, he was confronted by a bewildering array of baby clothes, accessories and toys. It didn't take him too long to find what he wanted, in the staffed-by-one and otherwise empty store. At the till, he spotted the name badge of 'Amanda' on the plump, middle-aged sales assistant. She greeted him in a friendly, broad Bristolian accent, and thanked him for his purchase.

"Been here long?" asked Mike.

"Oh, a little while. This shop has been open six months now, but we have had "Wonderland" for some time" replied Amanda, indicating with a nod of her head towards the next-door store. "But now I'm manager of both shops."

"Must keep you busy, then" remarked Mike.

"Oh yes, it does. Though I always have someone else also serving in one or the other."

Mike thanked her, and left swiftly, not wanting to let too much time slip way; as always, he was needing to be somewhere else.

He returned to his car and was soon driving up the road to the country park, and then into the rough ground which contained his special parking area for accessing the leisure trail. It was happily empty save for one other car. As he arrived, he saw a woman getting a pram out of the boot of the distinctive shiny red Mini Cooper S Countryman, who waved as she saw him appear.

Mike parked up and wandered over, by which time the pram was unfolded and the baby was now out of the car and in the woman's arms.

"Hi Mike; Carol is pleased to see you" proclaimed Ali, making a mock wave from her baby. "As I am, of course".

Mike moved in closer and they kissed and hugged for a long while. The Ali put Carol in the pram, and together they walked up along the path leading from the parking area, chatting as they walked. They stood side-by-side for a moment, looking out over the sweeping countryside view with the bridge in the distance.

"I got Carol a little something" pronounced Mike, with a shy smile, handing Ali small gift bag. The branding was at once familiar to Ali.

"You just bought this at my shop, you funny man" chuckled Ali. Pulling it out, she recognised it as a toy that could be suspended in the pram and dangled for the infant to play with.

"You and all things suspended, hey?" she exclaimed. "But actually, lovely, and just the thing to keep Carol amused". They kissed again, and then chatted some more.

Ali's plans had been turned upside down once she became pregnant. Her thoughts of opening the shop in Glasgow and moving there had been shelved for awhile, though certainly not cancelled; that was still her long-term aim. Instead, her new situation had led her to an enterprising conclusion. As she acquired knowledge of everything needed for a new baby, she figured that was an opportunity to market a new range of items. Then, when the unit next to her existing Bristol shop had come up for rent, she grabbed the opportunity to set up her new business. The deal was done when she had spoken with Amanda who had confirmed her willingness to manage both of the stores.

Meanwhile, Mike's altered situation had permitted him to lead with perfect double life. He had agreed with Joy that the move to Knutsford made sense for both of them, now that his work would pull him North and South, and she needed the support from her mother even more with a second child on the way. They secured a perfect property in a semi-rural location near the town and close to Joy's mother; and to Joy's, and her mother's, great pleasure, it came with an orchard of apple and plum trees.

Mike found that his new role transitioning the business was a slow, patient affair, which given his personal life suited him fine. When in Glasgow, he was put up in the impressive Millennium Hotel on George Square, over-looking the statues of Robert Burns, Sir Robert Pell and Sir Waler Scott. Though for Mike, James Watt was more to his interest, being a mechanical engineer and inventor. When in needed in the South, which was most weeks, Mike initially was in their house until it sold, and then in theory was staying in a hotel in Bristol. But most of the time he would stay with Ali in her cottage.

This arrangement meant that Mike could support both Joy and Ali through their pregnancies, though only Ali knew about Joy, and not the other way round. Ali was now even more keen to move to Glasgow eventually, where she and Mike could build a future together, but she could see the sense in delaying that until after she gave birth.

When the time came, Joy gave birth to a healthy baby boy that she named Edward. Only a couple of weeks later, Ali gave birth a beautiful girl she named Carol; continuing with the family humour that she thought her mother would have approved of; if it had been a boy, she would have gone for Lewis. Mike with some skilful planning and deception managed to be present for both births of his new children.

Now, three months later, Ali had her new shop business up and running in Bristol, and was keen to return her Northern expansion ideas, expecting that Mike would be changing to a full-time move to Glasgow at some point.

This weekend was a little different. Mike had convinced Joy that that a visit to his favourite cycling spot was in order, while she was busy staying in Knutsford celebrating her mother's birthday with some of her mum's friends. It pleased Joy's mother to see her grandchildren and not see Mike, so the arrangement worked for all of them.

An engine noise alerted Mike and Ali of someone else's arrival, so they turned around and pushed the pram back down the path, arriving in the car park to see two familiar occupants get out of a "Telecom Services" VW Passat estate.

"Hi Mike, Hi Ali" shouted Steve, who was now hand in hand with Julia, as the couples walked towards each other.

They kissed and hugged one another, and for awhile the focus was on baby Carol. Then Ali spied Julia's hand, and gasped. Julia, noticing the reaction, extended her fingers and beamed.

"You're looking at the future Mrs. Martin" announced Julia. Steve proposed last month, but we wanted to tell you in person.

"Wow, fantastic for both of you" Ali replied, leaning in for another kiss and hug.

"Congratulations" added Mike, shaking Steve's hand and giving his friend a light punch on the arm, before embracing Julia again.

Eventually, the boys got their bicycles out of their cars, and readied themselves.

"I will definitely come with you for a ride next time" promised Ali. "I'm not quite ready for it yet, but I will be"

"Well, in the meantime, we can catch up" suggested Julia. "And I can have some quality 'Aunty' time with little Carol here. I'm getting broody already."

A brief look of bewilderment flashed over Steve's face, at how fast things had been moving lately. Mike smiled at him. Without delay, Steve shot off on his bike up the trial.

"See you soon" called Mike to the girls, before riding off after Steve.

"No need to rush back" replied Ali, who was immediately in deep conversation with Julia.

As he caught him up, Mike whispered "Well done" to Steve, who nodded and replied: "You always tell me I should be bolder" Steve told him. "Well, this was the boldest move I ever made!"

Ali was pleased for Julia, but Julia was a little concerned for Ali, about the prospects of Mike leaving Joy. When Ali explained about the waiting until Joy was settled in the new house and the new baby, she was doubly concerned.

"Do you think he might be having second thoughts?" asked Julia. "If the marriage is over, then why doesn't he just tell her?"

"He says because he doesn't want to upset her, and keep good relations with his children, until it's the 'right time'" replied Ali, looking a little dejected. "Until then, he's trying to be her friend and help until everything is sorted. Which should be soon now. Meanwhile, we've been managing the situation ok."

Julia shook her head, and looking at Carol, replied: "But he has family with you now. He needs to make his decision and act upon it!" she exclaimed.

Meanwhile, Steve was similarly concerned for his old friend, given the crazy 'double life' Mike was leading. After a short ride, they paused for a moment to take in the view.

"So come on then" started Steve. "What are you doing about Ali? Surely you can't want to stay with Joy?"

"Yeah, well, it's complicated" replied Mike. I needed to get Joy and the boys sorted. It takes time to end a marriage. I know I need to face up to the future eventually."

"Weren't you the one who used to say 'Marriages should be like business contracts, and only last 10 years'?" reminded Steve.

Mike stared out across view, and as he did so, the sun broke out from the clouds, shining a shaft of light down on the Clifton suspension bridge, which reflected it back, shining brilliantly. A smile crept across his face, as he turned to Steve.

"You know, you've just given me an idea" Mike slowly responded.

"Oh, no, what now" replied Steve. "I know what you're like; you're going to act first and think later!"

"Hang on, just suspend beliefs for a moment; then the opportunities reveal themselves" Mike cryptically continued.

"Sounds like your usual crazy brain working overtime, but ok then, what?" Steve humoured his old friend.

"Just like a long-term business, what I need in my personal life is … is, a 10-year deal!" Mike concluded.

"What? What deal? You're not making any sense, man" Steve replied, exasperated. "How does that help to sort out the here-and-now?"

"You'll see! I just know, everything's going to turn out just fine …

About the author

Ben Sydney lives in the United Kingdom, with a professional career in industry.
This book provides a first fictional tale, a departure from previous non-fiction activities. Requiring a more imaginative and creative emphasis, the author found this enjoyable and stimulating to write, and hopes you will find it equally interesting and entertaining to read.

Next

Sequel to "Suspended Beliefs"
(to be written, hopefully, sometime soon):

10-YEAR DEAL

Ben Sydney

Bristol, Knutsford, Glasgow. Three children. Two women. One really good friend. A double-life that needs to be resolved. With decisions for work and home of where and with whom he is going to build a future. And a plan to sort everything out. Can Mike find a way to please everyone? Take a firm grip of his responsibilities and be bold enough to make everything all right? And live happily ever after. Or at least, for another 10-years?

If you would like to read this next story or something else, please make contact to provide your feedback and suggestions.

bensydneyauthor@gmail.com